PUFFI.

THE ADVENTURES OF FELUDA
TROUBLE IN GANGTOK

Satyajit Ray (1921–92) was one of the greatest filmmakers of his time, renowned for films like *Pather Panchali*, *Charulata*, *Aranyer Din Ratri* and *Ghare Baire*. He was awarded the Academy Honorary Award for Lifetime Achievement by the Academy of Motion Picture Arts and Science in 1992, and in the same year, was also honoured with the Bharat Ratna.

Ray was also a writer of repute, and his short stories, novellas, poems and articles, written in Bengali, have been immensely popular ever since they first began to appear in the children's magazine *Sandesh* in 1961. Among his most famous creations are the master sleuth Feluda and the scientist Professor Shonku.

*

Gopa Majumdar has translated several works from Bengali to English, the most notable of these being Ashapurna Debi's *Subarnalata*, Taslima Nasrin's *My Girlhood* and Bibhutibhushan Bandyopadhyay's *Aparajito*, for which she won the Sahitya Akademi Award in 2001. She has translated several volumes of Satyajit Ray's short stories and all of the Feluda stories for Penguin Books India. She is currently translating Ray's Professor Shonku stories, which are forthcoming in Puffin.

READ THE OTHER ADVENTURES OF FELUDA IN PUFFIN

SATYAJIT RAY'S
THE ADVENTURES OF FELUDA

TROUBLE IN GANGTOK

PUFFIN BOOKS

An imprint of Penguin Random House

PUFFIN BOOKS

USA | Canada | UK | Ireland | Australia
New Zealand | India | South Africa | China

Puffin Books is part of the Penguin Random House group of companies
whose addresses can be found at global.penguinrandomhouse.com

Published by Penguin Random House India Pvt. Ltd
7th Floor, Infinity Tower C, DLF Cyber City,
Gurgaon 122 002, Haryana, India

First published in Puffin by Penguin Books India 2003
This edition published in Puffin Books by Penguin Random House India 2019

ISBN 9780143335641

Typeset in Garamond Book by Manipal Technologies Limited, Manipal
Printed at Replika Press Pvt. Ltd, India

www.penguin.co.in

CHAPTER 1

Even a little while ago it had been possible to stare out of the window and look at the yellow earth, criss-crossed with rivers that looked like silk ribbons and sweet little villages with tiny little houses in them. But now grey puffs of cloud had blocked out that scene totally. So I turned away from the window and began looking at my co-passengers in the plane.

Next to me sat Feluda, immersed in a book on space travel. He always read a lot, but I had never seen him read two books—one straight after the other— that were written on the same subject. Only yesterday, back at home, he had been reading something about the Takla Makan Desert. Before that, he had finished a book on international cuisine, and another of short stories. It was imperative, he'd always maintained, for a detective to gain as much general knowledge as possible. Who knew what might come in handy one day?

There were two men sitting diagonally opposite me. One of them was barely visible. All I could see was his right hand and a portion of his blue trousers. He was beating one of his fingers on his knee. Perhaps he was singing quietly. The other gentleman sitting closer to us had a bright and polished look about him. His greying hair suggested he might be in his mid-forties, but apart from that he seemed pretty well preserved. He was reading the *Statesman* with great concentration. Feluda might have been able to guess a lot of things about the man, but I couldn't think of anything at all although I tried very hard.

'What are you gaping at?' Feluda asked under his breath, thereby startling me considerably. Then he cast a sidelong glance at the man and said, 'He's not as flabby as he might have been. After all, he does eat a lot, doesn't he?'

Yes, indeed. Now I remembered having seen him ask the air hostess for two cups of tea in the past hour, with which he had eaten half a dozen biscuits.

'What else can you tell me about him?' I asked curiously.

'He's used to travelling by air.'

'How do you know that?'

'Our plane had slipped into an air pocket a few minutes ago, remember?'

'Oh yes. I felt so strange! My stomach began to churn.'

'Yes, and it wasn't just you. Many other people around us had grown restless, but that gentleman didn't even lift his eyes from his paper.'

'Anything else?'

'His hair at the back is tousled.'

'So?'

'He has not once leant back in his seat in the plane. He's sat up straight throughout, either reading or having tea. So obviously at Dum Dum—'

'Oh, I get it! He must have had some time to spare at Dum Dum airport, at least time enough to sit back against a sofa and relax for a while. That's how his hair got tousled.'

'Very good. Now you tell me which part of India he comes from.'

'That's very difficult, Feluda. He's wearing a suit and he's reading an English newspaper. He could be a Bengali, a Punjabi, a Gujarati or a Maharashtrian, anything!'

Feluda clicked his tongue disapprovingly. 'You'll never learn to observe properly, will you? What's he got on his right hand?'

'A news—no, no, I see what you mean. He's wearing a ring.'

'And what does the ring say?'

I had to screw up my eyes to peer closely. Then I saw that in the middle of the golden ring was inscribed a single word: 'Ma'. The man had to be a Bengali.

I wanted to ask Feluda about other passengers, but at this moment there was an announcement to say that we were about to reach Bagdogra. 'Please fasten your seat belts and observe the no-smoking sign.'

We were on our way to Gangtok, the capital of Sikkim. We might have gone to Darjeeling again, where we had been twice already to spend our summer holidays. But at the last minute Feluda suggested a visit to Gangtok, which sounded quite interesting. Baba had to go away to Bangalore on tour, so he couldn't come with us. 'You and Felu could go on your own,' Baba told me. 'I'm sure Felu could take a couple of weeks off. Don't waste your holiday in the sweltering heat of Calcutta.'

Feluda had suggested Gangtok possibly because he had recently read a lot about Tibet (I too had read a travelogue by Sven Hedin). Sikkim had a strong Tibetan influence. The king of Sikkim was a Tibetan, Tibetan monks were often seen in the gumphas in Sikkim, many Tibetan refugees lived in Sikkimese villages. Besides, many aspects of Tibetan culture—their music, dances, costumes and food—were all in evidence in Sikkim. I jumped at the chance to go to Gangtok. But then, I would have gone anywhere on earth, quite happily, if I could be with Feluda.

Our plane landed at Bagdogra at 7.30 a.m. Baba had arranged a jeep to meet us here. But before climbing into it, we went to the restaurant at the airport to have breakfast. It would take us at least six hours to reach Gangtok. If the roads were bad, it might take even longer. However, since it was only mid-April, hopefully heavy rains hadn't yet started. So the roads ought to be in good shape.

I had finished an omelette and just started on a fish fry, when I saw the same gentleman from the plane rise from the next table and walk over to ours, grinning broadly. 'Are you Kang, or Dang, or Gang?' he asked, wiping his mouth with a handkerchief.

I stared, holding a piece of fish fry a few inches from my mouth. What on earth did this man mean? What language was he speaking in? Or was it some sort of a code?

But Feluda smiled in return and replied immediately, 'We're Gang.'

'Oh good. Do you have a jeep? I mean, if you do, can I come with you? I'll pay my share, naturally.'

'You're welcome,' said Feluda, and it finally dawned on me that Kang meant Kalimpong, Dang was Darjeeling, and Gang was Gangtok. I found myself laughing too.

'Thank you,' said the man. 'My name is Sasadhar Bose.'

'Pleased to meet you, Mr Bose. I am Pradosh Mitter and this is my cousin, Tapesh.'

'Hello, Tapesh. Are you both here on holiday?'

'Yes.'

'I love Gangtok. Have you been there before?'

'No.'

'Where will you be staying?'

'We're booked somewhere, I think the hotel is called Snow View,' Feluda replied, signalling at the waiter for our bill, and offering a Charminar to Mr Bose. Then he lit one himself.

'I know Gangtok very well,' Mr Bose told us. 'In fact, I've travelled all over Sikkim—Lachen, Lachung, Namche, Nathula, just name it! It's really beautiful. The scenery is just out of this world, and it's all so peaceful. There are mountains and rivers and flowers—you get orchids here, you know—and bright sunshine and rain and mist . . . nature in all her glory. The only thing that stops this place from being a complete paradise is its roads. You see, some of the mountains here are still growing. I mean, they are still relatively young, and therefore restless. You know what youngsters are like, don't you . . . ha ha ha!'

'You mean these mountains cause landslides?'

'Yes, and it can really be a nuisance. Halfway through your journey you may suddenly find the road completely blocked. That then means blasting your way through rocks, rebuilding the road, clearing up the mess . . . endless problems. But the army here is always on the alert and it's very efficient. Besides, it hasn't yet started to rain, so I don't think we'll have any problem today. Anyway, I'll be very glad of your company. I hate travelling alone.'

'Are you here on holiday as well?'

'Oh no,' Mr Bose laughed, 'I am here on business. But my job is rather a peculiar one. I have to look for aromatic plants.'

'Do you run a perfumery?'

'Yes, that's right. Mine's a chemical firm. Among other things, we extract essences from plants. Some of the plants we need grow in Sikkim. I've come to collect them. My business partner is already here. He arrived a week ago. He's got a degree in botany and knows about plants. I was supposed to travel with him, but a nephew's wedding came up. So I had to go to Ghatshila to attend it. I returned to Calcutta only last night.'

Feluda paid the bill. We picked up our luggage and began walking towards our jeep with Mr Bose.

'Where are you based?' Feluda asked.

'Bombay. This company is now twenty years old. I joined it seven years ago. S. S. Chemicals. Shivkumar Shelvankar. The company is in his name.'

We set off in a few minutes. From Bagdogra we had to go to Siliguri, to find Sewak Road. This road wound its way through the hills, going up and down. It would finally take us to a place called Rongpo, where West Bengal ended, and the border of Sikkim began.

On our way to Rongpo, we had to cross a huge bridge over the River Tista. On the other side was a market called Tista Bazaar. We stopped here for a rest. By this time the sun had come up, and we were all feeling a little hot.

'Would you like a Coca-Cola?' asked Mr Bose. Feluda and I both said yes, and got out of the jeep. 'Two years ago,' said Mr Bose, 'this whole area had been wiped out in a devastating flood. All the buildings and other structures, including the bridge, were new.'

By the time I finished my own bottle of Coca-Cola, Mr Bose had emptied two. When we went to return the bottles, we noticed a jeep parked near the stall selling cold drinks. A few men were standing near it, talking excitedly. The jeep had come from the other side, and was probably going to Siliguri. Suddenly, all of us caught the word 'accident', and went across to ask them what had happened. What they told us was this: It had rained heavily in Gangtok a week ago. Although there had been no major landslide, somehow a heavy boulder had rolled off a mountain and fallen on a passing jeep, killing its passenger. The jeep had fallen into a ravine, five hundred feet below. It was totally destroyed. None of these men knew who the dead man was.

'Fate,' said Feluda. 'What else can you call this? The man was destined to die, or else why should just a single boulder slip off a mountain and land on his jeep? Such accidents are extremely rare.'

'One chance in a million,' said Mr Bose. As we got back into the jeep, he added, 'Keep an eye on the mountains, sir. One can't be too careful.' However, the scenery became so incredibly beautiful soon after we crossed Tista that I forgot all about the accident. There was a brief shower as we were passing through Rongpo. As we climbed up to three thousand feet, a mist rose from the valley just below, making us shiver in the cold. We stopped shortly to pull out our woollens from our suitcase. I saw Mr Bose dig out a blue pullover from an Air India bag and slip it on.

Slowly, through the mist, I began to notice vague outlines of houses among the hills. Most houses appeared to be Chinese in style. 'Here we are,' said Mr Bose. 'It took us less than five hours. We're very lucky.'

The city of Gangtok lay before us. Our jeep made its way carefully through its streets, past a military camp, sweet little houses with wooden balconies and flower pots, groups of men and women in colourful clothes, and finally drew up before Snow View Hotel. The people in the streets, I knew, were not from Sikkim alone. Many of them were from Nepal, Bhutan or Tibet.

Mr Bose said he was staying at the dak bungalow. 'I'll make my own way there, don't worry,' he said. 'Thank you so much. No doubt we shall meet again. In a small place like this, it is virtually impossible to avoid bumping into one another every day.'

'Well, since we don't know anyone in Gangtok except you, I don't think we'd find that a problem. If you don't mind, I'll visit your dak bungalow this evening,' said Feluda.

'Very well. I'll look forward to it. Goodbye.'

With a wave of his hand, Mr Bose disappeared into the mist.

CHAPTER 2

Although our hotel was called Snow View and the rooms at the rear were supposed to afford a view of Kanchenjunga, we didn't manage to see any snow the day we arrived, for the mist didn't clear at all. There appeared to be only one other Bengali gentleman among the other guests in the hotel. I saw him in the dining hall at lunch time, but didn't get to meet him until later.

We went out after lunch and found a paan shop. Feluda always had a paan after lunch, though he admitted he hadn't expected to find a shop here in Gangtok. The main street outside our hotel was quite large. A number of buses, lorries and station wagons stood in the middle of the road. On both sides were shops of various kinds. It was obvious that business people from almost every corner of India had come to Sikkim. In many ways it was like Darjeeling, except that the number of people out on the streets was less, which helped keep the place both quiet and clean.

Stepping out of the paan shop, we were wondering where to go next, when the figure of Mr Bose suddenly emerged from the mist. He appeared to be walking hurriedly in the direction of our hotel. Feluda waved at him as he came closer. He quickened his pace and joined us in a few seconds.

'Disaster!' he exclaimed, panting.

'What happened?'

'That accident . . . do you know who it was?'

I felt myself go rigid with apprehension. The next words Mr Bose spoke confirmed my fears. 'It was SS,' he said, 'my partner.'

'What! Where was he going?'

'Who knows? What a terrible disaster, Mr Mitter!'

'Did he die instantly?'

'No. He was alive for a few hours after being taken to a hospital. There were multiple fractures. Apparently, he asked for me. He said, "Bose, Bose" a couple of times. But that was all.'

'How did you find out?' Feluda asked, walking back to the hotel. We went into the dining hall. Mr Bose sat down quickly, wiping his face with a handkerchief. 'It's a long story, actually,' he replied. 'You see, the driver survived. What happened was that when the boulder hit the jeep, the driver lost control. I believe the boulder itself wasn't such a large one, but because the driver didn't know where he was going, the jeep tilted to one side, went over the edge and fell into a gorge. The driver, however, managed to jump out in the nick of time. All he got was a minor cut over one eye. But by the time he could scramble to his feet, the jeep had disappeared with Shelvankar in it. This happened on the North Sikkim Highway. The driver began walking back to Gangtok. On his way he found a group of Nepali labourers who helped him to go back to the spot and rescue Shelvankar. Luckily, an army truck happened to be passing by, so they could take him to a hospital almost immediately. But ... well ...'

There was no sign of the jovial and talkative man who had accompanied us from Bagdogra. Mr Bose seemed shaken and deeply upset.

'What happened to his body?' Feluda asked gently.

'It was sent to Bombay. The authorities here got through to his brother there. SS had married twice, but both his wives are dead. There was a son from his first marriage, who fought with him and left home fourteen years ago. Oh, that's another story. SS loved his son; he tried very hard to contact him, but he had vanished without a trace. So his brother was his next of kin. He didn't allow a post-mortem. The body was sent to Bombay the next day.'

'When did this happen?'

'On the morning of the eleventh. He had arrived in Gangtok on the seventh. Honestly, Mr Mitter, I can hardly believe any of this. If only I was with him ... we might have avoided such a tragedy.'

'What are your plans now?'

'Well, there's no point in staying here any longer. I've spoken to a travel agent. I should be able to fly back to Bombay tomorrow.' He rose. 'Don't worry about this, please,' he added. 'You are here to have a good time, so I hope you do. I'll see you before I go.'

Mr Bose left. Feluda sat quietly, staring into space and frowning. Then he repeated softly the words Mr Bose had uttered this morning: 'One chance in a million . . . but then, a man can get struck by lightning. That's no less amazing.'

The Bengali gentleman I had noticed earlier had been sitting at an adjacent table, reading a newspaper. He folded it neatly the minute Mr Bose left, and came over to join us. 'Namaskar,' he said to Feluda, taking the chair next to him. 'Anything can happen in the streets of Sikkim. You arrived only this morning, didn't you?'

'Hm,' said Feluda. I looked carefully at the man. He seemed to be in his mid-thirties. His eyes were partially hidden behind tinted glasses. Just below his nose was a small, square moustache, the kind that was once known as a butterfly moustache. Not many people wore it nowadays.

'Mr Shelvankar was a most amiable man.'

'Did you know him?' Feluda asked.

'Not intimately, no. But from what little I saw of him, he seemed very friendly. He was interested in art. He bought a Tibetan statue from me only two days before he died.'

'Was he a collector of such things?'

'I don't know. I found him in the Art Emporium one day, looking at various objects. So I told him I had this statue. He asked me to bring it to the dak bungalow. When I showed it to him there, he bought it on the spot. But then, it was a piece worth having. It had nine heads and thirty-four arms. My grandfather had brought it from Tibet.'

'I see.' Feluda sounded a little stiff and formal. But I found this man quite interesting, especially the smile that always seemed to hover on his lips. Even the death of Mr Shelvankar appeared to have given him cause for amusement.

'My name is Nishikanto Sarkar,' he said.

Feluda raised his hands in a namaskar but did not introduce himself.

'I live in Darjeeling,' Mr Sarkar continued. 'We've lived there for three generations. But you'd find that difficult to believe, wouldn't you? I mean, just look at me, I am so dark!'

Feluda smiled politely without saying anything. Mr Sarkar refused to be daunted. 'I know Darjeeling and Kalimpong pretty thoroughly. But this is my first visit to Sikkim. There are quite a few interesting places near Gangtok, I believe. Have you already seen them?'

'No. We're totally new to Sikkim, like yourself.'

'Good,' Mr Sarkar grinned. 'You're going to be here for some time, aren't you? We could go around together. Let's visit Pemiangchi one day. I've heard it's a beautiful area.'

'Pemiangchi? You mean where there are ruins of the old capital of Sikkim?'

'Not just ruins, dear sir. According to my guide book, there's a forest, old dak bungalows built during British times, gumphas, a first-class view of Kanchenjunga—what more do you want?'

'We'd certainly like to go, if we get the chance,' said Feluda and stood up.

'Are you going out?'

'Yes, just for a walk. Is it necessary to lock up each time we go out?'

'Well, yes, that's always advisable in a hotel. But cases of theft are very rare in these parts. There is only one prison in Sikkim, and that's here in Gangtok. The total number of criminals held in there would be less than half a dozen!'

We came out of the hotel once more, only to find that the mist hadn't yet cleared. Feluda glanced idly at the shops and said, 'We should have remembered to buy sturdy boots for ourselves. These shoes would be no good if it rained and the roads became all slushy and slippery.'

'Couldn't we buy us some boots here?'

'Yes, we probably could. I'm sure Bata has a branch in Gangtok. We could look for it in the evening. Right now I think we should explore this place.'

The road that led from the market to the main town went uphill. The number of people and houses grew considerably less as we walked up this road. Most of the passers-by were schoolchildren in uniform. Unlike Darjeeling, no one was on horseback. Jeeps ran frequently, possibly because of the army camp. Sixteen miles from Gangtok, at a height of 14,000 feet, was Nathula. It was here that the Indian border ended. On the other side of Nathula, within fifty yards, stood the Chinese army.

A few minutes later, we came to a crossing, and were taken aback by a sudden flash of colour. A closer look revealed a man—possibly a European—standing in the mist, clad from head to foot in very colourful clothes: yellow shoes, blue jeans, a bright red sweater, through which peeped green shirt cuffs. A black and white scarf was wound around his neck. His white skin had started to acquire a tan. He had a beard which covered most of his face, but he appeared to be about the same age as Feluda—just under thirty. Who was he? Could he be a hippie?

He gave us a friendly glance and said, 'Hello.'

'Hello,' Feluda replied.

Now I noticed that a leather bag was hanging from his shoulder, together with two cameras, one of which was a Canon. Feluda too had a Japanese camera with him. Perhaps the hippie saw it, for he said, 'Nice day for colour.'

Feluda laughed. 'When I saw you from a distance, that's exactly what I thought. But you see, colour film in India is so expensive that one has to think twice before using it freely.'

'Yes, I know. But I have some in my own stock. Let me know if you need any.' I tried to work out which country he might be from. He didn't sound American; nor did he have a British or French accent.

'Are you here on holiday?' Feluda asked him.

'No, not really. I'm here to take photographs. I'm working on a book on Sikkim. I am a professional photographer.'

'How long are you going to be here for?'

'I came five days ago, on the ninth. My original visa was only for three days. I managed to have it extended. I'd like to stay for another week.'

'Where are you staying?'

'Dak bungalow. See this road on the right? The dak bungalow is on this road, only a few minutes from here.'

I pricked up my ears. Mr Shelvankar had also stayed at the same place.

'You must have met the gentleman who died in that accident recently—' Feluda began.

'Yes, that was most unfortunate,' the hippie shook his head sadly. 'I got to know him quite well. He was a fine man, and—' he broke off. Then he said, more or less to himself, 'Very strange!' He looked faintly worried.

'What's wrong?' Feluda enquired.

'Mr Shelvankar acquired a Tibetan statue from a Bengali gentleman here. He paid a thousand rupees for it.'

'One thousand!'

'Yes. He took it to the local Tibetan Institute the next day. They said it was a rare and precious piece of art. But—' The man stopped again and remained silent for a few moments. Finally, he sighed and said, 'What is puzzling me is its disappearance. Where did it go?'

'What do you mean? Surely his belongings were all sent back to Bombay?'

'Yes, everything else he possessed was sent to Bombay. But not that statue. He used to keep it in the front pocket of his jacket. "This is my mascot," he used to say, "it will bring me luck!" He took it with him that morning. I know this for a fact. When they brought him to the hospital, I was there. They took out everything from his pockets. There was a notebook, a wallet and his broken glasses in a case. But there was no sign of the statue. Of course, it could be that it slipped out of his pocket as he fell and is probably still lying where he was found. Or maybe one of those men who helped lift him out saw it and removed it from the spot.'

'But I've been told people here are very honest.'

'That is true. And that is why I have my doubts—' the man seemed lost in thought.

'Do you know where Mr Shelvankar was going that day?'

'Yes. On the way to Singik there's a gumpha. That is where he was going. In fact, I was supposed to go with him. But I changed my mind and left a lot earlier, because it was a beautiful day and I wanted to take some photographs here. He told me he'd pick me up on the way if he saw me.'

'Why was he so interested in this gumpha?'

'I'm not sure. Perhaps Dr Vaidya was partly responsible for it.'

'Dr Vaidya?'

This was the first time anyone had mentioned Dr Vaidya. Who was he?

The hippie laughed. 'It's a bit awkward, isn't it, to chat in the middle of the road? Why don't you come and have coffee with me in the dak bungalow?'

Feluda agreed readily. He was obviously keen to get as much information as possible about Shelvankar.

We began walking up the road on our right. 'Besides,' added the hippie, 'I need to rest my foot. I slipped in the hills the other day and sprained my ankle slightly. It starts aching if I stand anywhere for more than five minutes.'

The mist had started to clear. Now it was easy to see how green the surroundings were. I could see rows of tall pine trees through the thinning mist. The dak bungalow wasn't far. It was rather an attractive building, not very old. Our new friend took us to his room, and quickly removed piles of papers and journals from two chairs for us to sit. 'Sorry, I haven't yet introduced myself,' he said. 'My name is Helmut Ungar.'

'Is that a German name?' Feluda asked.

'Yes, that's right,' Helmut replied and sat down on his bed. Clearly, he didn't believe in keeping a tidy room. His clothes (all of them as colourful as the ones he was wearing) were strewn about, his suitcases were open, displaying more books and magazines than clothes, and spread on a table were loads of photographs, most of which seemed to have been taken abroad. Although my own knowledge of photography was extremely limited, I could tell these photos were really good.

'I am Pradosh Mitter and this is my cousin, Tapesh,' said Feluda, not revealing that he was an amateur detective.

'Pleased to meet you both. Excuse me,' Helmut went out of the room, possibly to order three coffees. Then he came back and said, 'Dr Vaidya is a very interesting person, though he talks rather a lot. He stayed here in this dak bungalow for a few days. He can read palms, make predictions about the future, and even contact the dead.'

'What! You mean he can act as a medium?'

'Yes, something like that. Mr Shelvankar was startled by some of the things he said.'

'Where is he now?'

'He left for Kalimpong. He was supposed to meet some Tibetan monks there. But he said he'd return to Gangtok.'

'What did he tell Mr Shelvankar? Do you happen to know anything about it?'

'Oh yes. They spoke to each other in my presence. Dr Vaidya told Mr Shelvankar about his business, the death of his wives, and about his son. He even said Mr Shelvankar had been under a lot of stress lately.'

'What could have caused it?'

'I don't know.'

'Didn't Shelvankar say anything to you?'

'No. But I could sense something was wrong. He used to grow preoccupied, and sometimes I heard him sigh. One day he received a telegram while we were having tea on the front veranda. I don't know what it said, but it upset him a good deal.'

'Did Dr Vaidya say that Mr Shelvankar would die in an accident?'

'No, not in so many words; but he did say Mr Shelvankar must be careful over the next few days. Apparently, there was some indication of trouble and bad times.'

The coffee arrived. We drank it in silence. Even if Mr Shelvankar's death had been caused truly by a freak accident, I thought, there was something wrong somewhere. It was evident that Feluda was thinking the same thing, for he kept cracking his knuckles. He never did this unless there was a nasty suspicion in his mind.

We finished our coffee and rose to take our leave. Helmut walked with us up to the main gate.

'Thank you for the coffee,' Feluda told him. 'If you're going to be here for another week, I'm sure we shall meet again. We're staying at the Snow View. Please let me know if Dr Vaidya returns.'

In reply, Helmut said just one thing: 'If only I could find out what happened to that statue, I'd feel a lot happier.'

CHAPTER 3

Although the mist had lifted, the sky was still overcast, and it was raining. I didn't mind the rain. It was only a faint drizzle, the tiny raindrops breaking up into a thin, powdery haze. One didn't need an umbrella in rain like this; it was very refreshing.

We found a branch of Bata near our hotel. Luckily, they did have the kind of boots we were looking for. When we came out clutching our parcels, Feluda said, 'Since we don't yet know our way about this town, we'd better take a taxi.'

'Where to?'

'The Tibetan Institute. I've heard they have a most impressive collection of tankhas, ancient manuscripts and pieces of tantric art.'

'Are you beginning to get suspicious?' I asked, though I wasn't at all sure that Feluda would give me a straight answer.

'Why? What should I be getting suspicious about?'

'That Mr Shelvankar's death wasn't really caused by an accident?'

'I haven't found a reason yet to jump to that conclusion.'

'But that statue is missing, isn't it?'

'So what? It slipped out of his pocket, and was stolen by someone. That's all there is to it. Killing is not so simple. Besides, I cannot believe that anyone would commit murder simply for a statue that had been bought for a thousand rupees.'

I said nothing more, but I couldn't help thinking that if a mystery did grow out of all this, it would be rather fun.

A row of jeeps stood by the roadside. Feluda approached one of the Nepali drivers and said, 'The Tibetan Institute. Do you know the way?'

'Yes, sir, I do.'

We got into the jeep, both choosing to sit in the front with the driver. He took out a woollen scarf from his pocket, wrapped it round his neck and turned the jeep around. Then we set off on the same road which had brought us into town. Only this time, we were going in the opposite direction.

Feluda began talking to the driver.

'Have you heard about the accident that happened recently?'

'Yes, everyone in Gangtok has.'

'The driver of that jeep survived, didn't he?'

'Yes, he's very lucky. Last year there had been a similar accident. The driver got killed, not the passenger.'

'Do you happen to know this driver?'

'Of course. Everyone knows everyone in Gangtok.'

'What is he doing now?'

'Driving another taxi. SKM 463. It's a new taxi.'

'Have you seen the accident spot?'

'Yes, it's on the North Sikkim Highway. Three kilometres from here.'

'Could you take us there tomorrow?'

'Yes, sure. Why not?'

'Well then, come to the Snow View Hotel at 8 a.m. We'll be waiting for you.'

'Very well, sir.'

A road rose straight through a forest to stop before the Tibetan Institute. The driver told us that orchids grew in this forest, but we didn't have the time to stop and look for them. Our jeep stopped outside the front door of the Institute. It was a large two-storey building with strange Tibetan patterns on its walls. It was so quiet that I thought perhaps the place was closed, but then we discovered that the front door was open. We stepped into a big hall. Tankhas hung on the walls. The floor was lined with huge glass cases filled with objects of art.

As we stood debating where to go next, a Tibetan gentleman, clad in a loose Sikkimese dress, came forward to meet us.

'Could we see the curator, please?' Feluda asked politely.

'No, I'm afraid he is away on sick leave today. I am his assistant. How may I help you?'

'Well, actually, I need some information on a certain Tibetan statue. I do not know what it's called, but it has nine heads and thirty-four arms. Could it be a Tibetan god?'

The gentleman smiled. 'Yes, yes, you mean Yamantak. Tibet is full of strange gods. We have a statue of Yamantak here. Come with me, I'll show it to you. Someone brought a beautiful specimen a few days ago—it's the best I've ever seen—but unfortunately, that gentleman died.'

'Oh, did he?' Feluda feigned total surprise.

We followed the assistant curator and stopped before a tall showcase. He brought out a small statue from it. I gasped in horror. Good heavens, was this a god or a monster? Each of its nine faces wore a most vicious expression. The assistant curator then turned it in his hand and showed us a small hole at the base of the statue. It was customary, he said, to roll a piece of paper with a prayer written on it and insert it through that little hole. It was called the 'sacred intestine'!

He put the statue back in the case and turned to us once more. 'That other statue of Yamantak I was talking about was only three inches tall. But its workmanship was absolutely exquisite. It was made of gold, and the eyes were two tiny rubies. None of us had ever seen anything like it before, not even our curator. And he's been all over Tibet, met the Dalai Lama—why, he's even drunk tea with the Dalai Lama, out of a human skull!'

'Would a statue like that be valuable? I mean, if it was made of gold—?'

The assistant curator smiled again. 'I know what you mean. This man bought it for a thousand rupees. Its real value may well be in excess of ten thousand.'

We were then taken on a little tour down the hall, and the assistant curator told us in great detail about some of the other exhibits. Feluda listened politely, but all I could think of was Mr Shelvankar's death. Surely ten thousand rupees was enough to tempt someone to kill? But then, I told myself firmly, Mr Shelvankar had not been stabbed or strangled or poisoned. He had died simply because a falling rock had hit his jeep. It had to be an accident.

As we were leaving, our guide suddenly laughed and said, 'I wonder why Yamantak has created such a stir. Someone else was asking me about this statue.'

'Who? The man who died?'

'No, no, someone else. I'm afraid I cannot recall his name, or his face. All I remember are the questions he asked. You see, I was very busy that day with a group of American visitors. They were our Chogyal's guests, so ...'

When we got back into the jeep, it was only five to five by my watch; but it was already dark. This surprised me since I knew daylight could not fade so quickly. The reason became clear as we passed the forest and came out into the open again. Thick black clouds had gathered in the western sky. 'It generally rains at night,' informed our driver. 'The days here are usually dry.' We decided to go back to the hotel as there was no point now in trying to see other places.

Feluda did not utter a single word on our way back. He simply stared out of the jeep, taking in everything he saw. If we went up this road again on a different day, I was sure he'd be able to remember the names of all the shops we saw. Would I ever be able to acquire such tremendous powers of observation, and an equally remarkable memory? I didn't think so.

We saw Mr Bose again as we got out of our jeep in front of our hotel. He appeared to be returning from the market, still looking thoughtful. He gave a little start when he heard Feluda call out to him. Then he looked up, saw us and came forward with a smile. 'Everything's arranged. I am leaving by the morning flight tomorrow.'

'Could you please make a few inquiries for me when you get to Bombay?' asked Feluda. 'You see, Mr Shelvankar had bought a valuable Tibetan statue. We must find out if it was sent to Bombay with his other personal effects.'

'All right, I can do that for you. But where did you learn this?'

Feluda told him briefly about his conversation with Mr Sarkar and the German photographer. 'Yes, it would have been perfectly natural for him to have kept the statue with him. He had a passion for art objects,' Mr Bose said. Then he suddenly seemed to remember something, and the expression on his face changed. He looked at Feluda again with a mixture of wonder and amusement.

'By the way,' he said, 'you didn't tell me you were a detective.'

Feluda and I both gave a start. How had he guessed? Mr Bose began laughing. Then he pulled out his wallet and, from it, took out a small visiting card. To my surprise, I saw that it was one of Feluda's. It said: Pradosh C. Mitter, Private Investigator.

'It fell out of your pocket this morning when you were paying the driver of your jeep,' Mr Bose told us. 'He picked it up and gave it to me, thinking it was mine. I didn't even glance at it then, but saw it much later. Anyway, I'm going to keep it, if I may. And here's my own card. If there is any development here . . . I mean, if you think I ought to be here, please send me a telegram in Bombay. I'll take the first available flight . . . Well, I don't suppose I'll meet you tomorrow. Goodbye, Mr Mitter. Have a good time.' Mr Bose raised his hand in farewell and began walking briskly in the direction of the dak bungalow. It had started to rain.

Feluda took his shoes off the minute we got back into our room and threw himself down on his bed. 'Aaaah!' he said. I was feeling tired too. Who knew we'd see and hear so many different things on our very first day?

'Just imagine,' Feluda said, staring at the ceiling, 'what do you suppose we'd have done if a criminal had nine heads? No one could possibly sneak up to him and catch him from behind!'

'And thirty-four arms? What about those?'

'Yes, we'd have had to use seventeen pairs of handcuffs to arrest him!'

It was raining quite hard outside. I got up and switched on the lights. Feluda stretched out an arm and slipped his hand into his handbag. A second later, he had his famous blue notebook open in front of him and a pen in his hand. Feluda had clearly made up his mind that there was indeed a mystery somewhere, and had started his investigation.

'Can you tell me quickly the name of each new person we have met today?'

I wasn't prepared for such a question at all, so all I could do for a few seconds was stare dumbly at Feluda. Then I swallowed and said, 'Today? Every new person? Do I have to start from Bagdogra?'

'No, you idiot. Just give me a list of people we met here in Gangtok.'

'Well . . . Sasadhar Datta.'

'Wrong. Try again.'

'Sorry, sorry. I mean Sasadhar Bose. We met him at the airport in Bagdogra.'

'Right. Why is he in Gangtok?'

'Something to do with aromatic plants, didn't he say?'

'No, a vague answer like that won't do. Try to be more specific.'

'Wait. He came here to meet his partner, Shivkumar Shelvankar. They have a chemical firm. Among other things, they . . .'

'OK, OK, that'll do. Next?'

'The hippie.'

'His name?'

'Helmet—'

'No, not Helmet. It's Helmut. And his surname?'

'Ungar.'

'What brought him here?'

'He's a professional photographer, working on a book on Sikkim. He had his visa extended.'

'Next?'

'Nishikanto Sarkar. Lives in Darjeeling. No idea what he does for a living. He had a Tibetan statue which he—'

I was interrupted by a knock on the door. 'Come in!' Feluda shouted.

The man I was just talking about walked into the room. 'I hope I'm not disturbing you?' asked Nishikanto Sarkar. 'I just thought I'd tell you about the Lama dance.'

'Lama dance? Where?' Feluda offered him a chair. Mr Sarkar took it, that same strange smile still hovering on his lips.

'In Rumtek,' he said, 'just ten miles from here. It's going to be a grand affair. People are coming from Bhutan and Kalimpong. The chief Lama of Rumtek— he is number three after the Dalai Lama—was in Tibet all this while. He has just returned to Rumtek. And the monastery is supposed to be new and worth seeing. Would you like to go tomorrow?'

'Not in the morning. Maybe after lunch?'

'OK. Or if you wish to have a darshan of His Holiness, we could go the day after tomorrow. I could get hold of three white scarves.'

'Why scarves?' I asked.

Mr Sarkar's smile broadened. 'That is a local custom. If you wish to meet a high-class Tibetan, you have to present him with a scarf. He'll take it from you, and return it immediately. That's all, that takes care of all the formalities.'

'No, I don't think we need bother about a darshan,' said Feluda. 'Let's just go and see the dance.'

'Yes, I would actually prefer that myself. The sooner we can go the better. You never know what might happen to the roads.'

'Oh, by the way, did you tell anyone else apart from Shelvankar about that statue?'

Mr Sarkar's reply came instantly, 'No. Not a soul. Why do you ask?'

'I was curious, that's all.'

'I did think of taking it somewhere to have it properly valued, but I met Mr Shelvankar before I could do that, and he bought it. Mind you, he didn't pay me at once. I had to wait until the next day.'

'Did he pay you in cash?'

'No, he didn't have that much cash on him. He gave me a cheque. Look!' Mr Sarkar took out a folded cheque from his wallet and showed it to Feluda. I leant over and saw it too. It was a National and Grindlays Bank cheque. Feluda returned it to Mr Sarkar.

'Did you notice anything sus-suspicious?' Mr Sarkar asked, still smiling. I realized later that he had a tendency to stammer if he was upset or excited. 'No, no.' Feluda yawned. Mr Sarkar rose to go. At this precise moment, there was a bright flash of lightning, followed almost immediately by the ear-splitting noise of thunder. Mr Sarkar went white. 'I can't stand thunder and lightning, heh heh. Good night!' He went out quickly.

It continued to rain throughout the evening. Even when I went to bed after dinner, I could hear the steady rhythm of the rain, broken occasionally by distant thunder. Despite that, it didn't take me long to fall asleep.

I woke briefly in the middle of the night and saw a figure walk past our window. But who would be mad enough to go out on a night like this? Perhaps I wasn't really awake. Perhaps the figure wearing a red garment that I saw only for a few seconds in the flash of lightning was no more than a dream . . . a figment of my imagination.

CHAPTER 4

I woke at 6.30 a.m. the next morning, to find that the rain had stopped and there was not a single cloud in the sky. The sun shone brightly on the world, and behind the range of mountains, now easily visible from our room, stood Kanchenjunga. The view from here was different from that in Darjeeling, but it was still unmistakably the same Kanchenjunga, standing apart from all the other mountains—proud, majestic and beautiful.

Feluda had risen before me and already had a bath. 'Be quick, Topshe. We have lots to do,' he said. It took me less than half an hour to get ready. By the time we went down for breakfast, it was only a little after 7 a.m. To our surprise, we found Mr Sarkar already seated in the dining hall.

'Good morning. So you're an early riser too,' Feluda greeted him.

Mr Sarkar smiled, but seemed oddly preoccupied, even somewhat nervous. 'Er . . . did you sleep well?' he asked.

'Not too badly. Why, what's the matter?'

Mr Sarkar glanced around briefly before taking out a crumpled yellow piece of paper from his pocket. Then he handed it over to Feluda and said, 'What do you make of this?'

Feluda spread it out. There were some strange letters written with black ink. 'It looks like a Tibetan word. Where did you get it?'

'Last night . . . in the . . . I mean, d-dead of night . . . someone threw it into my room.'

'What!' My heart gave a sudden lurch. Mr Sarkar's room was next to ours. The same stretch of the veranda that ran in front of our room went past his. If the man I saw last night was real, and not something out of a dream, why, he might have—! But I chose not to say anything.

'I wish I knew what it said,' added Mr Sarkar.

'That shouldn't be a problem, surely? Dozens of people here can read Tibetan. You could go to the Tibetan Institute, if no one else will help you. But why are you assuming this is some sort of a threat? It could simply mean "May you live long", or "God be with you", or something like that. Is there a specific reason to think this is a warning or a threat?'

Mr Sarkar gave a little start, then smiled and said, 'No, no, certainly not. I do nothing but mind my own business. Why should anyone threaten me? But then again, why should anyone send me their good wishes? I mean, purely out of the blue like this?'

Feluda called a waiter and ordered breakfast. 'Stop worrying. We're right next to you, aren't we? We'll both look after you. Now, have a good breakfast, relax and think of the Lama dance this afternoon.'

Our jeep arrived on time. Just as we were about to get into it, I saw another jeep coming from the direction of the dak bungalow. As it came closer, I could read its number plate. SKM 463, it said. Why did it seem familiar? Oh, of course, this was the new jeep that Mr Shelvankar's driver was now driving. I caught a glimpse of the blue jacket the driver was wearing, and then, to my utter surprise, I saw Mr Bose sitting in the passenger's seat. He stopped his jeep at the sight of ours. 'I was waiting for information from the army,' he told us, leaning out. 'All that rain last night made me wonder if the roads were all right.'

'And are they?'

'Yes, thank God. If they weren't, I'd have had to go via Kalimpong.'

'Didn't Mr Shelvankar use the same driver?'

Mr Bose laughed. 'I can see you've started making inquiries already. But yes, you're right. I chose him deliberately, partly because his jeep is new, and partly because . . . lightning doesn't strike the same place twice, does it? Anyway, goodbye again!'

He drove off and soon disappeared. We climbed into our own jeep. The driver knew where he was supposed to take us, so we were off without wasting another minute. I glanced up as we approached the dak bungalow to see if I could see Helmut, but there was no one in sight. There was a slope to our left, leading to another street lined by buildings. One of them looked like a school for there was an open square ground in front of it with two tiny goal posts. A little later, we reached a crossing where four roads met. We drove straight ahead and soon came across a large sign that said, 'North Sikkim Highway'.

Feluda had been humming under his breath. Now he broke off and asked the driver, 'How far has this road gone?'

'Up to Chungtham, sir. Then it splits into two—one goes to Lachen, and the other to Lachung.'

I had heard of both these places. They were both at a height of nearly 9,000 feet and reported to be very beautiful.

'Is it a good road?'

'Yes, sir. But it gets damaged sometimes after heavy rain.'

The few buildings that could be seen by the road soon disappeared altogether. We were now well out of the town, making our way through hills. Looking down at the valley below, I could only see maize fields. It seemed as though someone had cut steps in the hillside to plant the maize. It looked most attractive.

After driving in silence for another ten kilometres, our driver slowed down suddenly and said, 'Here's the spot. This is where the accident took place.' He parked the jeep on one side and we got out. The place was remarkably quiet. I could hear nothing but the faint chirping of a bird, and the gurgling of a small river in the far distance.

On our left was a slope. The hill rose almost in a straight line on our right. It was from the top of this hill that the boulder had fallen. Pieces of it were still strewn about. The thought of the accident suddenly made me feel a little sick.

Feluda, in the meantime, had finished taking a few quick photos. Then he passed his camera to me and walked over to the edge of the road on the left. 'It may be possible to climb down this slope, if I go very carefully. Wait for me. I shouldn't take more than fifteen minutes,' he said. Before I could say or do anything to stop him, he had stepped off the road and was climbing down the slope, clutching at plants, bushes and rocks, whistling nonchalantly. But the sound of his whistling faded gradually, and in just a few minutes there was silence once more. Unable to contain myself, I moved towards the edge of the road and took a quick look. What I saw made me give an involuntary gasp. I could see Feluda, but he had climbed such a distance already that his figure looked like that of a tiny doll.

'Yes, he's found the right spot,' said the driver, joining me. 'That's where the jeep had fallen.'

Exactly fifteen minutes later, I heard Feluda climbing up, once again clutching and grasping whatever he could lay his hands on. When he came closer, I stretched an arm and helped him heave himself up on the road.

'What did you find, Feluda?'

'Just some nuts and bolts and broken parts of a vehicle. No Yamantak.'

This did not surprise me. 'Did you find nothing else?' I asked. In reply, Feluda took out a small object from his pocket. It was a white shirt button, possibly made of plastic. Feluda put it away, and made his way to the hill that rose high on the other side of the road. I heard him mutter 'rocks and boulders, rocks and boulders' a couple of times. Then he raised his voice and said, 'Felu Mitter must now turn into Tenzing.'

'What do you mean? Why Tenzing? Hey Feluda, wait for me!'

This time, I was determined not to be left behind. The hill that had looked pretty daunting at first turned out to have little clefts and hollows one could use as footholds. 'All right, you go before me,' Feluda said. I knew he wanted to be right behind me so that he could reach out and catch me if I slipped and fell. Luckily, that did not happen. A few minutes later, I heard Feluda say, 'Stop!' We had reached a place that was almost flat. I decided to sit on a small rock and rest for a while. Feluda began pacing, examining the ground carefully. I paid no attention until he stopped and said, 'Hm. This is where that boulder must have slipped from. Look at those bushes over there—and that small fern—see how they've been crushed?'

'How big do you think it was?'

'You saw the pieces, didn't you? It need not have been very big. A rock the size of a dhobi's bundle would be enough to kill, if it fell from such a height.'

'Really?'

'Yes. It's a matter of momentum, you see. Mass into velocity. If you stood at the bottom of Qutab Minar and someone threw a pebble aimed at your head from its top, you might end up with a fractured skull. Haven't you noticed when you play cricket that the higher the cricket ball is thrown in the air, the more difficult and painful it is for a fielder to catch it?'

'Yes, I see what you mean.'

Feluda turned and started to stare at a certain spot that looked more barren than its surroundings. There were grassy patches everywhere else.

'Topshe, do you want to find out how that stone slipped out? Come and have a look.' Feluda pointed at something in that barren portion of the hill. I got up and peered. There was a small hole. What could it mean?

'As far as I can see,' Feluda said slowly, 'yes, I am almost a hundred per cent sure about this—someone forced the rock out of the ground, using either a strong iron rod, or something like that. Otherwise there wouldn't be an empty space here. Which means—'

I knew what his next words were going to be. But I held my breath and let him finish.

'—Which means the accident that took Mr Shelvankar's life was caused by man, not nature. Someone killed him ... someone incredibly cruel, and clever.'

CHAPTER 5

When we returned to the hotel from the place of
the murder (I am not going to call it an accident
any more), Feluda told me to wait in the hotel. He had
to go out on some work. I didn't ask him for details for
I knew he wouldn't tell me.

On our way back, we had met Helmut near the big
crossing. When he heard we were going to Rumtek later
in the afternoon, he said he'd like to join us. Nobody
had told him about the Lama dance. I wondered where
Mr Sarkar was. Had he managed to find out what that
Tibetan word meant?

I found him in the dining hall, looking morose and
depressed. However, my arrival seemed to cheer him
up. 'Where's your cousin?' he asked with his usual smile.

'He's gone out for a while. He should be back soon.'

'Er . . . he's very strong, isn't he?'

I looked up in surprise at this question, but Mr Sarkar continued, 'You see, I am staying on in Gangtok only because he said he'd help me, if need be. Or else I'd have gone back to Darjeeling today.'

'Why?'

Mr Sarkar began looking nervous again. Then he slowly took out the same yellow paper from his pocket. 'I've ne-never done anyone any harm. Why should anyone try to threaten me?'

'Did you find out what that word means?'

'Ye-es. I took it to the Tibetan Institute. And they said . . . they said it means "death". Giangphung, or something like that. The Tibetan word for death. It's got me really worried. I am thirty-seven now, you see, and once an astrologer had told me my stars were all going to fall into unfavourable positions after I turned thirty-seven . . .'

This irritated me somewhat. 'I think you are jumping to conclusions,' I said a little sternly. 'All it says is "death". Does it say you have to die?'

'Yes, yes, you're right. It could be anybody's death, couldn't it? Even so . . . I don't know . . .' I thought of the figure in red I had seen last night. But obviously it was better not to mention it to Mr Sarkar. He was upset enough as it was. After a few moments of silence, he seemed to pull himself together with an effort. 'I mustn't brood,' he said. 'Your cousin's there to help me. The very sight of him inspires confidence. Is he a sportsman?'

'He used to play cricket. Now he does yoga.'

'I knew it! One doesn't often get to see a man looking so fit. Anyway, would you like a cup of tea?'

I was feeling quite tired after all that climbing. So I said yes, and Mr Sarkar ordered tea for both of us. Feluda arrived just as the waiter placed two steaming cups before us. Mr Sarkar told him of his problem at once. Feluda looked at the Tibetan word again and asked, 'Can you figure out why anyone should want to do this to you?'

'No, sir. I've thought a great deal, but I can't think of a reason at all.'

'Very well. If you're sure there's no one to bear you a grudge, then there's nothing to be worried about. I am sure that was dropped into your room by mistake. What is the point in threatening someone in a language he doesn't know? That warning must have been meant for someone who can read Tibetan. You were not the real target.'

'Yes, that makes a lot of sense. Besides, I can rely on you, can't I, if there's any trouble?'

'Yes, but perhaps there's something I should tell you here and now. Trouble follows me around wherever I go.'

'R-really?'

Feluda went up to our room without another word. I knew he couldn't stand people who were given to frequent attacks of nerves. If Mr Sarkar wanted his support, he'd have to stop whining all the time.

When I returned to our room after finishing my tea, Feluda was writing something in his blue notebook. 'I knew most people in telegraph offices were illiterate, but this is too much!' he exclaimed upon seeing me.

'Why, what happened?'

'I sent a telegram to Mr Bose. He will get it as soon as he reaches Bombay.'

'What did you tell him?'

'Have reason to suspect Shelvankar's death not accidental. Am investigating.'

'But why are you so cross with the telegraph office?'

'That's another matter. You see, I went to find out if Shelvankar had received any telegrams while he was here. It wasn't easy to get this information, of course, but in the end they told me there had been two. One was from Mr Bose, saying, "Am arriving fourteenth."'

'And the other?'

'Here, read this,' Feluda offered me his notebook. I saw what was written in it: YOUR SON MAY BE IS A SICK MONSTER. PRITEX.

I stared. What on earth did it mean? Were we now going to deal with demons and monsters?

'Some words have clearly been misspelt. But what could they be?' Feluda muttered.

'What is Pritex?'

'That probably refers to a private detective agency.'

'You mean Shelvankar had appointed a detective to trace his son?'

'Quite possibly. But "sick monster"? Dear God!'

'This is getting increasingly complicated, Feluda. How many mysteries will you solve all at once?'

'I was thinking the same thing. There is no end to the questions. In fact, it might not be a bad idea to write them down.' He bent over his notebook, pen in hand.

'Go ahead,' he invited.

'Number one—sick monster.'

'Yes. Next?'

'Who threw that boulder?'

'Good.'

'Number three—where did that statue disappear?'

'Carry on. You're doing quite well.'

'Number four—who threw that piece of paper into Mr Sarkar's room?'

'And why? All right, next?'

'Number five—whose shirt button did you find at the site of the murder?'

'Yes, although that might well have dropped from the shirt of the murder victim.'

'Number six—who, apart from ourselves, went to the Tibetan Institute to ask about Yamantak?'

'Splendid. If you keep going like this, in about ten years you'll become a full-fledged detective yourself!'

I knew Feluda was joking, but I felt quite pleased to think I had passed the test.

'There is only one person we haven't yet met and I feel we ought to.'

'Who is that?'

'Dr Vaidya. If he can make predictions for the future, speak to departed souls, and perform other tricks, he's got to be an interesting man.'

CHAPTER 6

We left for Rumtek as planned, taking the road to Siliguri. The same road turned right to join a new road that went straight up to Rumtek. Both roads passed through picturesque villages and green and gold maize fields. I found the ride thoroughly enjoyable, despite the fact that the sun had disappeared and the sky had started to turn grey.

Our driver was driving very cautiously. Feluda and I sat with him in the front. Helmut and Mr Sarkar sat at the back, facing each other. Helmut's foot, he said, was now a lot better. The pain had gone, thanks to a German pain balm he had used. Mr Sarkar seemed much more cheerful. I could hear him humming a Hindi song. Only Feluda was totally silent and withdrawn. I knew he was trying very hard to find answers to those six questions. If we hadn't already planned this trip, he would have spent the afternoon scribbling in his notebook.

Our jeep turned right, bringing into view new houses and buildings, and rows of what looked like bunting. I learnt later that Tibetans hung square pieces of cloth from ropes outside their houses in the belief that they ward off evil spirits.

A few minutes later, a faint noise that had already reached my ears grew louder. It was a mixture of the deep and sombre sound of a horn, clanking of cymbals and a shrill note from a flute. This must be the music for the Lama dance, I thought, as our jeep pulled up outside the huge gate of the monastery. 'The Lamas are dan-dancing,' informed Mr Sarkar, possibly for Helmut's benefit. All of us climbed out.

Passing through the gate, we found ourselves in a large open courtyard. A beautiful blue-and-white embroidered shamiana stood over it. The audience sat under the shamiana. About ten men, wearing bright costumes and rather grotesque masks, were dancing before this audience, jumping and swaying to the music. The musicians were all dressed in red. Small boys— barely ten years old—were blowing the horns, each one of which was several feet long. I had never seen anything like it.

Helmut started taking photos. He was carrying three cameras today.

'Would you like to sit down?' asked Mr Sarkar.

'What do you want to do?' Feluda said.

'I have seen this kind of thing before, in Kalimpong. I'm going to have a look at the temple behind this courtyard. Its inside walls are supposed to be beautifully carved.'

Mr Sarkar left. Feluda and I sat down on the floor. 'Tradition is a strange thing,' remarked Feluda. 'A traditional dance like this can make you forget you're living in the twentieth century. I don't think this form of dance has changed at all in the last thousand years.'

'Why is this place called a gumpha?'

'No, this isn't a gumpha. A gumpha is a cave. This is a monastery. See those little rooms on the other side? That's where the monks stay. All these little boys with shaved heads, wearing long Tibetan robes are being trained to become monks. In a monas—' Feluda broke off. I looked at him quickly to find him frowning, his mouth hanging open. Now, what was the matter? What had he suddenly thought of? 'It's this mountain air,' he said finally, shaking his head. 'It's affecting my brain. I've stopped thinking. Why did it take me so long to work out what that telegram meant? It's so simple!'

'How is it simple? I still can't—'

'Look, it said "sick". That means Sikkim. And "monster" is monastery.'

'Hey, that makes sense! What does the whole thing say?'

'YOUR SON MAY BE IS A SICK MONSTER. If you read "IN" for "IS", it says YOUR SON MAY BE IN A SIKKIM MONASTERY.'

'Does that mean Mr Shelvankar's son, who left home fifteen years ago, is here right now?'

'That's what Pritex said. If Shelvankar had managed to figure out the meaning of this telegram, he might well have started to feel hopeful. From what I've heard, he loved his son and wanted him back.'

'Perhaps he was going to that gumpha the day he died only to look for his son.'

'That's entirely possible. And if his son was really somewhere in Sikkim, the chances of ...' Feluda broke off again. Then I heard him mutter under his breath, 'Will ... will ... if Shelvankar made a will leaving everything to his son, he stood to gain a lot.' Feluda rose and made his way out of the crowd. I followed quickly. He was obviously feeling restless, having just discovered what the telegram had really meant. I saw him look around. Was he looking for an Indian among the Tibetans?

We began walking in the direction of the temple, where Mr Sarkar had disappeared a few minutes ago. There were fewer people on the other side of the courtyard. As we passed the rooms in which the monks lived, we saw a couple of very old monks sitting outside in the corridor, turning a prayer wheel silently, their eyes closed. If their heavily wrinkled faces were anything to go by, they must have been a hundred years old.

Behind the rooms was a long veranda. Its walls were covered with pictures depicting scenes from the Buddha's life. The veranda led to a dark hall. Inside it, flickering oil lamps stood in rows. A huge wooden door, painted red, had been thrown open, but there was no one at the door. Feluda and I stepped in quietly.

The dark, damp hall was filled with a strange scent of incense. Incredibly long lengths of bright silk, heavily embroidered, hung from the high ceiling. Benches, draped in colourful fabrics, stood in corners, as did what looked like very large drums. These were supported by bamboo rods. Behind these, in the darkest corner of the hall, were a number of tall statues, chiefly of the Buddha. Flowers had been arranged in a number of vases, and the oil lamps I had seen from outside were placed under the statues.

I was totally engrossed in looking at these things when suddenly Feluda placed a hand on my shoulder. I looked up swiftly and found him staring at a side entrance to the hall. A much smaller door on one side was open.

'Let's get out of here,' he said, speaking through clenched teeth, and started to move towards the door.

We emerged from the hall to find a flight of stairs going up. 'I can't tell where he went, but let's go upstairs, anyway,' Feluda said.

'Where who went?' I whispered, running up the stairs.

'A man in red. He was peeping into the hall. Ran away the moment he realized I had seen him.'

'Did you see his face?'

'No, it was too dark.'

We found a room on the first floor, but its door was closed. Perhaps this was the senior Lama's room, who had recently returned from Tibet. On the left was an open terrace. Here again, pieces of cloth hung from ropes. Strains of the music from the courtyard down below reached my ears. A dance like this could go on for seven or eight hours.

We walked across the terrace and stood by a railing, overlooking a green valley. A mist had started to rise, slowly engulfing everything that was visible. 'If Shelvankar's son was here—' Feluda began, but was interrupted by a loud scream.

'Help me! Oh God . . . save! . . . help . . . help!'

It was Mr Sarkar's voice.

We ran back to the stairs. It took us less than a minute to get down and find the rear exit from the monastery. We rushed out to find that the shrieks for help were coming from the bottom of a hill. The area was uneven, dotted with bushes and shrubs, one end leading to a steep drop of about a hundred feet. It was here that Mr Sarkar was hanging from a bush, right at the edge of the hill. Our appearance made him shout even louder. 'I am d-d-dying . . . save me, please save me!'

It wasn't too difficult to pull him up to safety. But the instant his feet touched solid ground, he rolled his eyes and fainted. Then we had to carry him back to the jeep and splash cold water on his face. He came round in a few moments and sat up slowly.

'What happened?' asked Feluda.

'D-don't remind me!' Mr Sarkar whimpered. 'After that long journey, I n-n-needed to . . . I mean . . . relieve myself, you see . . . so I thought I'd better go out of the monastery, and I found this place that seemed quite suitable, but . . . but who knew I had been followed?'

'Did someone give you a push from the back?'

'Absolutely. It was h-horrible! If I hadn't found that bush to hang on to, that Tibetan warning would have come t-true, in no t-time!'

'Did you see the man?'

'No, of course not! He stole up behind me, didn't he?'

There was no point in staying on in Rumtek after an incident like this. We decided to go back to Gangtok immediately. Helmut, who had seen us coming back to the jeep, agreed to return with us, although I suspect he was disappointed at not being able to take more photos.

Feluda had sunk into silence once more. But he spoke suddenly as our driver started the jeep. 'Mr Sarkar,' he said, 'surely you realize you have a certain responsibility in this whole business?'

'Res-responsibility?' croaked Mr Sarkar.

'There's no way we can figure out who's trying to frighten you unless you tell us what—or whom—you are after.'

Mr Sarkar sat up, looking profoundly distressed. 'I swear, sir—I promise—I've never caused anyone any harm. Not knowingly, anyway.'

'You don't happen to have an identical twin, do you?'

'No, no. I am the only child of my parents.'

'Hm. I assume you're telling the truth. Mind you, if you tell me a lie, it is you who is going to be in trouble.'

The rest of the journey was made in total silence. Feluda spoke again only when our jeep stopped at the dak bungalow and Helmut tried to pay his share.

'No, no,' Feluda said, 'we invited you, didn't we? Besides, you are a guest in our country. We cannot allow you to pay a single paisa.'

'All right.' Helmut smiled. 'Will you at least allow me to offer you a cup of tea?'

This seemed like a very good idea, so all of us got out. Feluda and Mr Sarkar paid the driver. Helmut then took us to his room.

We had just found three chairs for ourselves, and Helmut had placed his cameras on the table, when a strange man walked into the room and greeted Helmut with a smile. A thick beard—flecked with grey—covered most of his face. Long hair came down to his shoulders. He was clad in loose flannel trousers and a shapeless orange jacket with a high neck. In his hand was a stout walking stick.

Helmut smiled back, and turned to us. 'Allow me to introduce you,' he said. 'This is Dr Vaidya.'

CHAPTER 7

'A re you from Bengal?' Dr Vaidya asked. He spoke
with a funny accent.

'Yes,' Feluda replied. 'Helmut has told us about you.'

'Helmut is a nice boy,' Dr Vaidya nodded, 'but I've had
to warn him about one thing. People here don't normally
like being photographed. You see, it is their belief that
if a part of a person is represented somewhere else in a
different form, it reduces the vital force—the ability to
live—of that person.'

'Do you believe this yourself?'

'What I believe is of no consequence, at least not
to Helmut. He hasn't stopped taking pictures, has he?
Why, I have been captured in his camera too! What I say
is this: One cannot disregard anything in life without
studying it, or examining it thoroughly. I still have a lot
to learn.'

'But there's such a lot you know already! I've heard you can see the future and even speak to the dead.'

'No, not always.' Dr Vaidya gave a slight smile. 'A lot depends on the immediate surroundings. But there are certain things that are fairly easy to tell. For instance, I can tell that this gentleman here is under a lot of stress,' he pointed at Mr Sarkar, who licked his lips nervously.

'Yes, you're right,' Feluda said. 'Somebody is trying to threaten him. He thinks his life is in danger. Can you tell us who is doing this?'

Dr Vaidya closed his eyes. He opened them a few seconds later and stared out of the window absently. 'Agent,' he said.

'Agent?'

'Yes. A man must be punished for his sins. Sometimes he is punished by the Almighty. At other times, God sends His agents out to do this job.'

'Enough!' shouted Mr Sarkar. His voice shook. 'I don't want to hear any more.'

Dr Vaidya smiled again. 'I am saying all this only because your friend asked me. If you can learn something yourself, there's no need to go looking for a teacher. But one thing I must tell you. If you wish to live, you will have to tread most carefully.'

'What does that mean?' asked Mr Sarkar.

'I can't say anything more than that.'

The tea arrived. Helmut poured it out and passed the cups around.

'I believe you met Mr Shelvankar,' said Feluda, sipping his tea.

'Yes. It's all very sad. I did warn him about a rough patch he might have to go through. But death? No, that's a different matter altogether, and no one has any control over it.'

No one spoke after this. We drank our tea in silence. Helmut sorted a few papers out on his table. Mr Sarkar stared absently into space, apparently unaware that his tea was getting cold. Only Feluda seemed totally at ease, happily finishing the biscuits that had arrived with the tea. After a while, Helmut rose to switch on a light. Daylight had almost gone by this time. But it turned out that there was a power cut. 'I'll get some candles,' said Helmut and went out to look for the bearer.

Feluda turned to Dr Vaidya again. 'Do you really believe Mr Shelvankar's death was accidental?'

Dr Vaidya took a moment to reply. Then he said, 'Only one person knows the answer to that question.'

'Who?'

'The person who died. Only he knows the truth. We who are living look upon this world and this life through eyes that take in every irrelevant and unnecessary detail. Just look out of that window. All those mountains and trees and rivers are irrelevant. They stand as a screen between ourselves and the truth. But death opens an inner eye that sees nothing but what is real and of true significance.'

Most of this speech went over my head, but I was sure Feluda had understood every word. 'You mean it is only Mr Shelvankar who could tell how he died?' Feluda asked.

'Yes. He couldn't have known the truth when he died. But now . . . yes, now he knows exactly what happened.'

I shivered suddenly. There was something eerie in the atmosphere, in so much talk about death, and the way Dr Vaidya smiled in the dark. It gave me goose pimples.

The bearer came in at this moment. He cleared the table and placed a candle on it. Feluda took out a packet of Charminar, offered it to everyone else in the room, then lit one himself. 'It may be a good idea to consult Mr Shelvankar and see what he thinks,' he remarked, blowing out a smoke ring. I knew he had read a lot on seances and most things supernatural. He kept an open mind on every subject, never hesitating to read or hear about other people's views, even if he didn't believe in something himself.

Dr Vaidya closed his eyes. A few moments later, he opened them and said, 'Shut the door and windows.' There was something authoritative in his tone. Mr Sarkar got up like a man hypnotized and obeyed silently. We were left sitting around the table in the faint flickering light of the candle. On my right was Dr Vaidya. On my left sat Feluda. Mr Sarkar sat next to him. Helmut finished the circle.

'Place your hands, palms down, on this table. Your fingers must touch your neighbour's,' commanded Dr Vaidya. We did as we were told. Dr Vaidya placed his own hands between mine and Helmut's, and said, 'Look straight at that candle and think of the death of Shelvankar.'

The candle was burning steadily. A few drops of wax had fallen on the table. A small insect, trapped in the room, began buzzing around the flame. God knows how long we sat in silence. I did cast a few sidelong glances at Dr Vaidya, but he couldn't have seen me for his own eyes were closed.

After a long time, he spoke. His voice sounded very faint as though he was speaking from a great distance. 'What do you want to know?' he asked. Feluda answered him. 'Did Mr Shelvankar die in an accident?'

'No,' said that faint, strange voice.

'How did he die?'

Silence. All of us were now gazing at Dr Vaidya. He was leaning back in his chair. His eyes were shut tight. Lightning flashed outside, lighting up our room for a second. Feluda's question was answered the same instant.

'Murder,' said Dr Vaidya.

'Mu-h-h-u-rder?' Mr Sarkar gasped.

'Who killed him?' Feluda wanted to know. He was staring at Dr Vaidya's hands. Dr Vaidya sighed. Then he began breathing hard, as though the act of breathing was causing him a great deal of pain. 'Virendra!' he finally whispered. 'Virendra? Who was he?' Feluda started to speak, but Dr Vaidya opened his eyes unexpectedly and said, 'A glass of water, please.'

Helmut rose and poured him water from his flask. Feluda waited until Dr Vaidya had finished drinking it. Then he asked, 'I don't suppose there's any chance of finding out who this Virendra is?'

Helmut answered him this time. 'Virendra is Mr Shelvankar's son. He told me about him.'

It was now time for us to leave. All of us stood up. Helmut opened the door and windows. The power came back a second later.

'You get nervous rather easily, don't you?' said Dr Vaidya, placing a hand on Mr Sarkar's shoulder. Mr Sarkar tried to smile. 'Anyway, I don't think you are in any danger now,' Dr Vaidya told him reassuringly. This time, Mr Sarkar smiled more naturally, looking visibly relieved.

'How long are you here for?' Feluda asked Dr Vaidya.

'I'd like to go to Pemiangchi tomorrow, if it doesn't rain. I've heard they've got some ancient valuable manuscripts in the monastery there.'

'Are you making a study of Tibet and the Tibetan culture?'

'Yes, you might call it that. It's the only ancient civilization that's left in the world. Egypt, Iraq, Mesopotamia . . . each one of those got destroyed. But for that matter, what is left in India, tell me? It's all a great hotch-potch. It's only Tibet that's managed to retain most of what it had. Luckily, some of the old monasteries in Sikkim have got pieces of their art and culture, so one doesn't have to go all the way to Tibet to find them.'

We came out, to find that the sky was covered by thick, dark clouds, being frequently ripped by lightning. It was certain that it would start raining again.

'Why don't you go to Pemiangchi as well?' Dr Vaidya asked.

'Yes, we might do that. I've heard a lot about the place.'

'If you do, don't forget to take a bag of salt with you.'

'Salt? Whatever for?'

'Leeches. There's nothing like salt to get rid of them.'

CHAPTER 8

Feluda, Mr Sarkar and I were back in our hotel, sitting down to our dinner. Although the hotel was pretty average in many ways, it had an excellent cook.

'A most decent fellow, I must say,' remarked Mr Sarkar, trying to get the marrow out of a bone. A delicious lamb curry was on the menu tonight.

'Who? You mean Dr Vaidya?'

'Yes. What a remarkably gifted man too. He seemed to know everything.'

'Yes, you should be pleased,' Feluda said, laughing. 'Didn't he tell you you were no longer in danger?'

'Why, didn't you believe what he said?'

'If what he said turns out to be true, then of course I shall believe him. But, right now, I think we should be careful in what or whom we believe. There are so many cheats in this line.' Feluda was frowning again.

Something was obviously bothering him a great deal. I wish I knew what it was.

'Do you believe what he said about the murder?' Mr Sarkar persisted.

'Yes, I do.'

'Really? Why?'

'There is a reason.' Feluda refused to say anything more.

The two of us went out after dinner again to buy paan. It hadn't yet started to rain, but there was virtually no breeze. Feluda put a paan in his mouth and began pacing. After only a few minutes, however, he stopped and said, 'I'm only wasting my time like this. Tell you what, Topshe, why don't you go for a walk for half an hour? I'd like to work alone in our room, undisturbed.'

I agreed, and Feluda walked away. I ambled across to the opposite pavement and made my way slowly down the road that led to the main town. All the shops were closed. A few men were sitting in a circle in front of a shop and gambling. I heard someone rattle the dice, which was followed by a great shout and loud laughter.

The street lights were dim, but even so I didn't fail to notice the figure of a man coming from the opposite direction, walking very fast. As he came closer, I realized it was Helmut. Something stopped me from calling out to him. But he was so preoccupied that even when he passed me by, he didn't seem to notice me at all. I stared foolishly at his receding back, until it vanished from sight. Then I looked at my watch and returned to the hotel.

Feluda was lying flat on his back, resting his notebook on his chest.

'I brought the list of suspects up to date,' he told me as I came in.

'Well, Virendra Shelvankar was already a suspect, wasn't he? It's just that we didn't know his name. Have you added Dr Vaidya's name to your list?'

Feluda grinned. 'The man put up a jolly good show, I must admit. Yet, the whole thing could be genuine, who knows? But we mustn't forget that he and Shelvankar had talked to each other. There's no way of making sure whether Dr Vaidya is a fraud or not unless we can find out what exactly the two had discussed.'

'But he was right about Mr Sarkar, wasn't he?'

'That was easy enough. Mr Sarkar was biting his nails constantly. Anyone could have guessed he was tense.'

'And what about the murder?'

'He may have said that only to create an effect. A natural death, or death by a real accident, is too tame. Call it a murder, and it sounds so much more dramatic.'

'So who's on your list of suspects?'

'Everyone, as always.'

'Everyone including Dr Vaidya?'

'Yes. He may have known about the statue of Yamantak.'

'And Helmut? He walked past me just now, but didn't seem to see me.'

This did not appear to surprise Feluda. 'Helmut struck me as a mysterious character right from the start. He's supposed to be taking photographs for a book on Sikkim, and yet he didn't know about the Lama dance in Rumtek. That's reason enough to feel suspicious about him.'

'Why? What can it mean?'

'It can mean that he hasn't told us the real reason why he is here in Sikkim.' I began to feel quite confused, so I stopped asking questions. Feluda went back to scribbling in his notebook.

At a quarter to eleven, Mr Sarkar knocked on our door to say goodnight. I tried to read a book after that, but couldn't concentrate. Feluda spent his time either sitting silently or studying the entries in his notebook. I do not know when I fell asleep. When I woke, the mountains outside were bright with sunshine.

Feluda was not in the room. Perhaps he was having a shower. I noticed a piece of paper on his bed, placed under an ashtray. Had he left a message for me? I picked it up and found a Tibetan word staring at me. I knew what it meant.

Death.

CHAPTER 9

Feluda was not in the bathroom. I learnt later that he had risen early that morning to make a trunk call to Bombay. When I came down for breakfast, I found him speaking to someone on the telephone.

'I couldn't get Mr Bose,' he told me, putting the receiver down. 'He left very early this morning. Perhaps he got my telegram.'

We ordered breakfast. 'I'll have to conduct an experiment today,' Feluda revealed a few minutes later. 'I think I made a mistake somewhere. I have to make sure.'

'Where will you carry out this experiment?'

'I need a quiet spot.'

'You mean an empty room?'

'No, no, you idiot. I could use our hotel room if that's what I needed. I have to be out on the road, but I must not be seen. If anyone saw me, they'd definitely think I was mad. Let's go towards Nathula Road after breakfast.' We hadn't yet seen any of the other large streets of Gangtok. The prospect of doing a little more exploration on foot was quite exciting.

We ran into Dr Vaidya as we came out of the hotel. He was wearing sunglasses today. 'Where are you off to?' he asked.

'Just for a walk. We haven't really seen much of the city. We were thinking of going towards the palace.'

'I see. I am going to look for a jeep. It's a good day to make that trip to Pemiangchi. If you don't go there, you really will miss a lot.'

'We do intend going there one day.'

'Try to make it while I'm there. Gangtok isn't a very safe place, particularly for you.'

Dr Vaidya left with a smile and a friendly wave.

'Why did he say that?' he asked.

'He's a very clever man. He wanted to startle us, that's all. Clearly he's seen I am involved in a complex matter, so he decided to say something odd for more effect.'

'But you really have been threatened, haven't you? I saw that piece of paper.'

'That's nothing new, is it?'

'No, but—'

'But nothing. If you think I'll give up now simply because someone wrote a Tibetan word on a piece of paper, you don't know me at all.'

I didn't say anything, but thought to myself how well I did know him. Hadn't I seen him work wonders in the case of the emperor's ring in Lucknow, despite being showered with threats and warnings?

We had been walking uphill and had now reached a point where the road spread out, almost like the Mall in Darjeeling. There was a small roundabout with yellow roadsigns. The one pointing right said 'Palace'. There was a large, heavily decorated gate at the end of this road, which was obviously the gate of the palace. The sign on the left said 'Nathula Road'. It seemed a quiet enough road. The few people we could see all appeared to be tourists, heading for the palace. 'Let's take this left turn. Quick!' Feluda said.

We turned left and took the road that led to the Chinese border. There was no one in sight. Feluda kept looking up at the hills through which the road had been built. We had now come to the eastern side of Gangtok. Kanchenjunga was on the west. I couldn't see any of the snow-capped peaks from here, but what I could see was a ropeway.

It seemed so interesting that I stopped and stared at it, losing all track of time. I had to look up with a start a few minutes later, when I heard Feluda calling out to me. While I had been gazing at the busy ropeway, Feluda had climbed up the side of a hill, and was shouting from several feet above the road. 'Hey, Topshe, come here!'

I left the road and joined him. Feluda was standing near a rock, nearly as large as a football. 'I'm going down,' he said. 'I'll come walking past the hill. Push this stone down when I tell you to. Just a little push will make it roll off the hill. Is that clear?'

'Yes, sir. No problem!'

Feluda climbed down and disappeared in the direction from which I had come.

Then I heard him call, 'Ready?'

'Ready!' I replied.

Feluda started walking. I couldn't see him, but I heard his footsteps. A few moments later, he came vaguely within my line of vision, but before I could see him properly, I heard him shout, 'Go!' I pushed the rock, and it began to roll down. Feluda did not stop walking. By the time the rock landed on the road, he had crossed that area and gone ahead by at least ten steps.

'Wait right there!' he shouted again.

He then came back with the rock in his hand. It was still intact. 'Now you go down, and walk past this hill exactly as you saw me do. I will throw this stone at you, but you must continue walking. If you can see it rolling down at enormous speed and feel that it might hit you, you'll have to jump aside. Can you do that?'

'Sure.'

I scrambled down, and started walking, keeping an eye on Feluda. I saw him standing still, waiting for the right moment. Then he kicked the stone. I kept on walking. The stone hit the ground a few seconds before I could reach the spot. Then it rolled down the slope on the left and disappeared.

Feluda sat down, slapping his forehead. I didn't want to stand around like a fool, so I climbed up again.

'What an ass I've been, Topshe! What a perfect idiot. This simple—'

'Feluda!' I screamed, quickly pulling him to one side. In the same instant, a huge boulder came crashing from the top of the hill and went down, missing us by inches and crushing a large flowering bush on the way. By the time it struck the road and vanished from sight, my breathing was starting to return to normal. Thank God, I had looked up when Feluda was speaking. Thank God, I had seen the boulder. If I hadn't ... I shuddered to think of the consequences.

'Thanks, Topshe,' Feluda said. 'This place really appears unsafe. Let's go back.'

We got down to the road and walked as fast as we could to the next crossing. There were benches on one side, placed under a canopy. We threw ourselves down on one of these. 'Did you see anyone?' asked Feluda, wiping his face.

'No. That boulder came from quite a height. I couldn't have seen who threw it even if I had had the time to look.'

'I've got to move faster now. I've got to find a final solution!'

'But there are so many questions that need to be answered.'

'And who told you I haven't found some of the answers already? Do you know what time I went to bed last night? At 2 a.m. I did a lot of thinking. And now this experiment merely confirmed every suspicion I had. Mr Shelvankar's jeep had not been hit by a falling rock. One cannot commit a murder banking on a chance that's one in a million. What really happened, I'm sure, was this: Mr Shelvankar was knocked unconscious. Then he was dropped into that ravine, along with the jeep. Someone pushed that boulder afterwards, just to make it look an accident.'

'But the driver? What about him?'

'He had been bribed. I'm sure of it.'

'Or the driver himself might have killed him?'

'No, that's unlikely. He wouldn't have had a sufficiently strong motive.'

Feluda rose. 'Let's get back, Topshe. We must find SKM 463.'

But SKM 463 was not in Gangtok, as it turned out. It had left for Siliguri the day before. 'I think people want to hire it because it's a new jeep,' Feluda remarked.

'What do we do now?'

'Wait, let me think. I'm getting muddled.'

We returned to the hotel from the jeep stand. Feluda ordered cold drinks in the dining hall. His hair was dishevelled and he seemed greatly perturbed.

'When did we arrive here?' he asked suddenly.

'Fourteenth April.'

'And when was Shelvankar killed?'

'On the eleventh.'

'Apart from Shelvankar, Mr Sarkar was here in Gangtok, and Helmut and Dr Vaidya.'

'And Virendra.'

'All right, let us make that assumption. When did Mr Sarkar get that Tibetan warning?'

'On the night of the fourteenth.'

'Right. Who was in town that day?'

'Helmut, Mr Bose, Virendra, and ... and ...'

'Mr Sarkar.'

'Yes, of course.'

'He may well have committed a crime. Maybe he is trying to remove suspicion from himself by showing us a piece of paper with a Tibetan word written on it.

He may have written it himself. His shrieks for help in Rumtek could have been a clever piece of acting.'

'But what can he have done?'

'I don't know that yet, though I don't think he killed Shelvankar.'

'Well then, who is left?'

'Dr Vaidya. Don't forget him. We don't know for sure whether he did go to Kalimpong or not.'

Feluda finished a glass of Sikkim orange in one gulp. Then he continued, 'The only person whose movements cannot be questioned is Mr Bose, because he came with us and went to Bombay the next day. Someone in his house confirmed that he had indeed returned to Bombay. But he's not there now. Maybe he's on his way here. Perhaps our trip to Pemiangchi—' Feluda stopped speaking. Someone had walked into the dining hall and was talking to the manager. It was our German friend, Helmut Ungar. The manager pointed at us. Helmut wheeled around. 'Oh, sorry, I didn't realize you were here,' he said, adding rather hesitantly, 'There's something I'd like to discuss with you. Do you think we could go up to your room?'

CHAPTER 10

'May I close the door?' asked Helmut as we walked into our room. Then he shut the door without waiting for an answer. I looked at him and began to feel vaguely uneasy. He was tall and strong, taller than Feluda by at least an inch. What did he want to do that required such secrecy? I had heard that some hippies took drugs. Was Helmut one of them? Would he—?

By this time, Helmut had placed his camera on my bed, and was opening a large red envelope with Agfa written on it.

'Would you like a cup of tea?' Feluda offered.

'No, thanks. I came here only to show you these photos. I couldn't get them printed here. So I had sent them to Darjeeling. I got the enlargements only this morning.'

Helmut took out the first photograph. 'This was taken from the North Sikkim Highway. The road where the accident took place goes right across to the opposite hill. You can get a wonderful view of Gangtok from there. That is where I was that morning, taking photos of this view. Mr Shelvankar had offered to pick me up on his way. But his jeep never got to the spot where I was standing. I heard a noise as I was clicking, which made me turn around. What I saw from where I was standing has been captured in these photos that I took with my telephoto lens.'

It was a strange photo. Most of the details were clear, although it had been taken from a distance. A jeep was sliding down a hill. A few feet above it, a man was standing on the road, looking at the falling jeep. This was probably the driver. He was wearing a blue jacket. His face couldn't be seen.

Helmut took out the second photo. This was even stranger. Taken a few seconds after the first one, it showed the jeep lying wrecked by the side of the hill. Next to it, behind a bush, there was a partially hidden figure of a man in a dark suit, lying on the ground. The driver was still standing on the road, this time with his back to the camera, looking up at the hill. Right on top of the hill was another man, bending over a rock. His face was just as unclear, but he was wearing red clothes.

In the third photograph, this man in red could not be seen at all. The driver was running—in fact, he had nearly shot out of the frame. The jeep and the man in the dark suit were still lying on the ground. And the rock that was on top of the hill was now lying on the road, broken to pieces.

'Remarkable!' Feluda exclaimed. 'I have never seen photographs like these!'

'Well, it isn't often that one gets such an opportunity,' Helmut replied dryly.

'What did you do after taking these pictures?'

'I returned to Gangtok on foot. By the time I could walk across to the spot where the jeep had fallen, Mr Shelvankar had been taken away. All I could see was the broken jeep and the shattered rock. I heard about the accident the minute I reached Gangtok. I then went straight to the hospital where Mr Shelvankar had been taken. He remained alive for a couple of hours after I got there.'

'Didn't you tell anyone about the photographs?'

'No. There was no point, at least not until I could have the film developed, and use it as evidence. Yet, I knew it was not an accident, but murder. Had I been a little closer, the face of the murderer might have been clearer in the picture.'

Feluda took out a magnifying glass and began examining the large prints again. 'I wonder if that man in red is Virendra?' he said.

'That's impossible!' Helmut declared. There was something in his voice that made us both look at him in surprise.

'Why? How can you be so sure?'

'Because I am Virendra Shelvankar.'

'What!' For the first time, I saw Feluda go round-eyed.

'What do you mean? How can you be Virendra? You are white, you have blue eyes, you speak English with a German accent, your name . . .'

'Please let me explain. You see, my father married twice. My mother was his first wife. She was a German. She met my father in Heidelburg when he was a student. That was where they got married. Her maiden name was Ungar. When I left India and settled in Germany, I started using this name, and changed my first name from Virendra to Helmut.'

My head started reeling. Helmut was Shelvankar's son? Of course, if he had a German mother, that would explain his looks.

'Why did you leave home?' Feluda asked after a brief pause.

'Five years after my mother died, my father married again. I couldn't bring myself to accept this. I loved my mother very much. It's not that I did not care for my father, but somehow when he remarried, I began to hate him. In the end, I thought leaving home was the only thing I could do to solve my problems. It wasn't easy to travel to Europe on my own, and make a new beginning. For about eight years, I moved from place to place, and job to job. Then I studied photography, and finally started to make money. A few years ago, I happened to be in Florence working on an assignment. A friend of my father's saw me there and recognized me. He came back and told my father about it, after which he approached a detective agency to track me down. When I came to know about this, I grew a beard and changed the colour of my eyes.'

'Contact lenses?'

Helmut smiled and took the lenses out of his eyes. His real eyes were brown, just like my own. He then put the lenses back and continued, 'A year ago, I came to India with a group of hippies. I hadn't stopped loving this country. But then I realized that the detective agency was still trying to trace me. I went to a monastery in Kathmandu. When someone found me even there, I came over to Sikkim.'

'Wasn't your father pleased to see you?'

'He did not recognize me at all. I have lost a lot of weight since he last saw me. Besides, my long hair, my beard and blue eyes must have all worked together to stop him from recognizing his own son. He told me about Virendra, and how much he missed him. By this time, I too had forgotten my earlier dislike of my father. After all, whatever happened between us was now in the past. But when he failed to recognize me, I did not tell him who I was. I probably would have told him eventually, but . . . well, I never got the chance.'

'Do you have any idea who the murderer might be?'

'May I speak frankly?'

'Of course.'

'I don't think we should let Dr Vaidya escape.'

'I agree with you,' said Feluda, lowering his voice.

'I began to suspect him the minute he mentioned the name of Virendra that evening in my room. Obviously, he didn't know I was the same person. I think he is a first class cheat, and I bet it was he who took that statue.'

'When Mr Shelvankar set out that morning, was he alone?'

'I don't know. I left quite early, you see. Dr Vaidya may well have stopped the jeep on the way and asked for a lift. Naturally, at that stage, my father had no reason to suspect him. In any case, he was a simple man. He trusted everyone.'

Feluda stood up and began pacing. Then he stopped abruptly and said, 'Would you like to go to Pemiangchi with us?'

'Yes. I am prepared to go anywhere to catch my father's killer.'

'Do you know how far it is?'

'About a hundred miles from here. If the roads are good, we can get there in less than six hours. I think we should leave today, as soon as possible.'

'Yes, you're right. I'll try to find a jeep.'

'OK, and I'll get rooms booked at the dak bungalow in Pemiangchi. By the way—' Helmut turned back from the doorway, 'a dangerous man like him may well be armed. I have nothing except a flashgun. Do you—?'

Without a word, Feluda slipped a hand inside his suitcase and brought out his revolver. 'And here's my card,' he said, handing one of his cards to Helmut.

'Pradosh C. Mitter, Private Investigator', it said.

Unfortunately, we couldn't get a jeep that day. The few there were had all been hired by American tourists for a day trip to Rumtek. We booked one for the next morning and spent the day walking around in the streets of Gangtok.

We ran into Mr Sarkar near the main market. 'We're going to Pemiangchi tomorrow,' Feluda told him. 'Would you like to join us?'

'Oh sure. Thanks!'

In the evening, he came to our room carrying a strange object. A small white bundle was tied at the end of a stick. 'I bet you can't guess what this is,' he said, beaming. 'This is actually used to get rid of leeches. This small bundle contains salt and tobacco. If a leech attaches itself to your foot, just rub it once with this stick and it's bound to drop off.'

'But how can a leech attack anyone through heavy leather boots and nylon socks?'

'I don't know, but I've seen leeches slip through even very thick layers of clothes. The funny thing about leeches is that they can't see. Suppose a number of people were walking in single file, no leech would attack the person at the head of the file. It would simply pick up the vibrations created by his movements. Then it would get ready to strike as the second person passed it by; and for the third, there would be no escape at all. He would definitely get bitten.'

We decided to take four similar sticks with us the next day.

'It's Buddha Purnima the day after tomorrow,' Feluda remarked as we were getting ready for bed. 'There will be a big celebration here.'

'Shall we get to see it?'

'I don't know. But if we can catch the man who killed Mr Shelvankar, that will make up for everything we miss seeing.'

The sky remained clear that night. I spent a long time looking at a moon that was nearly full. Kanchenjunga gleamed in its light.

The next day, the four of us left for Pemiangchi at five in the morning, with just a few essentials. Mr Sarkar did not forget the 'leech-proof' sticks.

C H A P T E R   11

There were two routes to Pemiangchi. Unfortunately, we couldn't take the shorter one as the main road had been damaged. Taking the longer route meant spending at least eight hours on the journey. Pemiangchi was a hundred and twenty-seven miles away. But it couldn't be helped. Our hotel had given us packed lunches, and we had two flasks. One was full of hot coffee, the other had water. So there was no need for us to stop anywhere for lunch, which would have taken up a lot of time.

Helmut was carrying only one camera today. Mr Sarkar, I noticed, had packed a pair of galoshes. 'No point in taking risks,' he told me. 'This is cent per cent safe.'

'Cent per cent? What if a leech fell on your head from a tree?'

'No, that's not likely. That happens in July and August. Leeches are normally to be found on the ground at this time of the year.'

Mr Sarkar didn't know we were going in search of a criminal. He was therefore perfectly happy and relaxed.

We reached Singtham at a quarter past six. We had passed through this town on our way to Gangtok. A left turn brought us to the River Tista again. We crossed it and found ourselves on a road none of us knew. This led straight to Pemiangchi. The jeep we were in wasn't new, but was in reasonably good condition. Its driver looked like a bandit from a Western film. He was dressed purely in black—the trousers, shirt and the leather jerkin he wore were all black. Even the cap on his head was dark enough to qualify as black. He was too tall to be a Nepali, but I couldn't figure out where he was from. Feluda asked him his name. 'Thondup,' he replied.

'That's a Tibetan name,' said Mr Sarkar, looking knowledgeable.

We drove in silence for about twenty kilometres. The next town on the way to Pemiangchi was Namchi. Just as we got close to it, a jeep behind us started blowing its horn loudly. Thondup made no attempt to let it pass.

'Why is he in such a hurry?' Feluda asked.

'No idea, sir. But if we let it go ahead, it'll only blow up clouds of dust.'

Thondup increased his speed. But the sound of the horn from the other jeep got more insistent. Mr Sarkar turned around irritably to see who it was. Then he exclaimed, 'Why, look, it's that same gentleman!'

'Who?' Feluda and I turned and saw, to our amazement, that Mr Bose was in the other jeep, still honking and waving madly.

'You'll have to stop for a minute, Thondupji,' Feluda said. 'That's a friend of ours.'

Thondup pulled up by the side of the road. Mr Bose came bounding out of the other jeep. 'Are you deaf or what?' he demanded. 'I yelled myself hoarse in Singtham, but none of you heard me!'

'Sorry, very sorry, Mr Bose. If we knew you were back, we wouldn't have left without you,' Feluda apologized.

'I could hardly stay on in Bombay after receiving your telegram. I've been following your jeep for miles.'

Thondup was absolutely right about the dust. Mr Bose was covered with it from head to foot, like an ash-smeared sadhubaba, thanks—no doubt—to the wheels of our own jeep.

'In your telegram you said you were suspicious about something. So where are you off to now? Why did you leave Gangtok?'

Instead of giving him a straight answer, Feluda asked, 'Do you have a lot of luggage?'

'No, just a suitcase.'

'In that case, why don't we move our own luggage into your jeep, and you can climb in with us? I'll fill you in.'

It took only a couple of minutes to transfer all the luggage. Mr Bose climbed in at the back with Mr Sarkar and Helmut, and we set off again. Feluda told Mr Bose briefly what had happened over the last two days. He even revealed that Helmut was Mr Shelvankar's son.

Mr Bose frowned when Feluda finished. 'But who is this Dr Vaidya? He's bound to be a fraud. You should not have allowed him to get away, Mr Mitter. You could have—'

Feluda interrupted him. 'My suspicions fell on him when I learnt about Helmut's true identity. You are partly to blame, Mr Bose. You should have told us your partner's first wife was a German.'

'How was I to know that would matter? Besides, all I knew was that she was a foreigner. I had no idea about her nationality. Shelvankar married her about twenty-five years ago. Anyway, I just hope that Vaidya hasn't left Pemiangchi. Or our entire journey will come to nothing!'

We reached Namchi a little after ten. Here we stopped for a few minutes, to pour cold water into the engine, and hot coffee into ourselves. I could see clouds gathering in the sky, but wasn't unduly worried since I'd heard Namchi was considered by many to be the driest and cleanest place in Sikkim. Helmut was taking photographs, more out of habit than any real interest. He had hardly spoken since we left.

Now that Mr Sarkar had learnt the real reason for going to Pemiangchi, he seemed faintly uneasy; but the prospect of having an adventure was obviously just as appealing. 'With your cousin on one side, and the German Virendra on the other, I see no reason to worry,' he declared to me.

We left Namchi after ten minutes. The road went down from here, towards another river called Rangeet. This river was very different from the Tista. Its water was clear, with a greenish tinge, and it flowed with considerable force. Pools of foam formed where it struck against stones and rocks. I had never seen such a beautiful river in the hills. We had to cross another bridge and climb up the hill again to get to Pemiangchi, which was at a height of 9,000 feet.

As we wound our way up, I could see evidence of landslides almost everywhere. The thick green foliage on the hills had large gaps here and there. Great chunks of the hill had clearly slid down towards the river. Heaven knew how long it would take nature to repair the damage caused by these 'young mountains'!

We passed a gumpha on the way. Outside its entrance were a lot of flags strung from a thin rope, to ward off evil spirits. Each of them looked clean and fresh. 'Preparations for Buddha Purnima,' explained Mr Bose.

'When is it?' asked Feluda absent-mindedly.

'Buddha Purnima? Tomorrow, I think. On seventeenth April.'

'Seventeenth April . . . on the Indian calendar that would be the fourth of Baisakh . . . hmm . . . Baisakh . . .'

I looked at Feluda in surprise. Why was he suddenly so concerned about dates? And why was he looking so grim? Why was he cracking his knuckles?

There was no opportunity to ask him. Our jeep had entered a forest. The road here had been badly damaged by the recent rains. Thondup crawled along with extreme care, despite which there were a few nasty bumps. One of these resulted in Mr Sarkar banging his head against the roof of the jeep. 'Bloody hell!' I heard him mutter.

The forest grew thicker and darker. Helmut pointed at a tall tree with dark green leaves and a light bark, and said, 'That's a birch. If you ever went to England, you'd get to see a lot of them.' There were trees on both sides. The road coiled upwards like a snake. It wasn't just dark inside the forest, but also much more damp. From somewhere came the sharp cry of a strange bird.

'Th-thrilling, isn't it?' said Mr Sarkar. Suddenly, without any warning, the trees cleared. We found ourselves in front of a hillock, under an overcast sky. A few moments later, the tiled roof of a bungalow came into view, followed by the whole building.

This was the famous dak bungalow of Pemiangchi. Built during British times, it stood at a spot that was truly out of this world. Rows and rows of peaks rose behind the bungalow, their colours ranging from lush green to a hazy blue.

Our jeep stopped outside the front door. The chowkidar came out. On being told who we were, he nodded and confirmed that rooms had been booked for us.

'Is there anyone else staying here?' asked Mr Bose.

'No, sir. The bungalow's empty.'

'Empty? Why, did no one come here before us?' Feluda asked anxiously.

'Yes, but he left last night. A man with a beard, and he wore dark glasses.'

CHAPTER 12

The chowkidar's words appeared to disappoint Helmut the most. He sat down on the grass outside, placing his camera beside him.

Mr Bose said, 'Well, there's nothing we can do immediately, can we? Let's have lunch. I'm starving.'

We went into the bungalow carrying our luggage. It was obvious that the bungalow had been built several decades ago. The wooden floor and ceiling, the wide verandas with wooden railings and old-fashioned furniture all bore evidence of an era gone by. The view from the veranda was breathtaking. If the sky wasn't cloudy, we would have been able to see Kanchenjunga, which was twenty-two miles away. There was no noise anywhere except the chirping of birds.

We crossed the veranda and went into the dining hall. Mr Bose found an easy chair and took it. He said to

Feluda, 'I wasn't too sure about Vaidya before, although you did tell me you had your suspicions. But now I'm convinced he's our man. SS should never have shown him such a valuable object as that statue.'

Helmut had risen to his feet, but hadn't joined us. I could see him pacing in the veranda outside. Mr Sarkar went inside, possibly to look for a bathroom. Feluda began to inspect the other rooms in the bungalow. I sat quietly in the dining hall, feeling most depressed. Was our journey really going to turn out to be a complete waste of time?

There were two doors on one side, leading to two bedrooms. Feluda came out of one of these with a walking stick in his hand. 'Dr Vaidya most certainly visited this place,' Feluda said, 'and he left this stick to prove it. How very strange!' Feluda's voice sounded different. I looked up quickly, but said nothing. Mr Sarkar returned, wiping his face with a handkerchief. 'What a weird place!' he exclaimed, taking the chair next to mine, yawning noisily. Feluda did not sit down. He stood before the fireplace, tapping the stick softly on the ground. His mouth was set in a grim line.

'Mr Sarkar!' called Mr Bose. 'Where are those packed lunches your hotel gave you? Let's eat.'

'No!' said Feluda, his voice sounding cold and remote. 'This is not the time to eat.'

Mr Sarkar had started to rise. He flopped back in his chair at Feluda's words. Mr Bose and I both looked at him in surprise. But Feluda's face remained without expression.

Then he sat down, lit a Charminar and inhaled deeply. 'Mr Bose,' he said conversationally, 'you know someone in Ghatshila, you said. Isn't that where you were before you caught a flight from Calcutta?'

'Yes. A nephew of mine got married.'

'You are a Hindu, aren't you, Mr Bose?'

'Why? What do you mean?'

'You heard me. What are you? A Hindu, or a Muslim, or a Christian, or what?'

'How does that—?'

'Just tell me.'

'I'm a Hindu, of course.'

'Hm.' Feluda blew out two smoke rings. One of them wafted towards Mr Bose, getting larger and larger, until it disappeared in front of his face.

'But,' Feluda frowned, 'you and I travelled together in the same plane. You had just got back from Ghatshila, hadn't you?'

'Yes, but why is that causing you such concern? I can't understand this at all, Mr Mitter. What has my nephew's wedding in Ghatshila got to do with anything?'

'It has plenty to do with things, Mr Bose. Traditionally, no Hindu would get married in the month of Chaitra. We left Calcutta on fourteenth April, which was the first of Baisakh. Your nephew's wedding took place before that, so it must have been in the preceding month, which was Chaitra. How did you allow this to happen?'

Mr Bose was in the middle of lighting a cigarette. He stopped, his hands shaking a little. 'What are you implying, Mr Mitter? Just what are you trying to say?'

Feluda looked steadily at Mr Bose, without giving him an immediate answer. Then he said, slowly and deliberately, 'I am implying a lot of things, Mr Bose.

To start with, you are a liar. You never went to Ghatshila. Secondly, you betrayed someone's trust—'

'What the hell is that supposed to mean?' Mr Bose shouted.

'We have all heard how depressed Mr Shelvankar had been before he died. He had even mentioned it to Helmut, though he did not specify the reason. It is easy enough to get totally broken in spirit if one is betrayed by a person one has trusted implicitly. I believe you were that person. You were his partner, weren't you? Mr Shelvankar was a simple, straightforward man. You took full advantage of this and cheated him endlessly. But one day, he came to know of what you had done. When you realized this, you decided to get him out of the way forever. That wasn't possible in Bombay, so you had to wait until he came to Sikkim. You were not supposed to be here. But you came—possibly the next day—disguised as Dr Vaidya. Yes, you were Dr Vaidya! You met Shelvankar and impressed him a great deal by telling him a few things about his life that you knew already. Then you told him about the possibility of finding Virendra in a gumpha, and left with him that morning in the same jeep. On the way, you hit his head with this heavy stick. This made him unconscious, but he did not die. You went ahead with your plan, and had the jeep pushed into the gorge. The driver had, no doubt, been bribed; that must have been easy enough to do. Then you threw that stone from the hill, using the same heavy stick to dislodge it from the ground. In spite of all this, Mr Shelvankar remained alive for a few hours, long enough to mention your name. Perhaps he had recognized you at the last minute.'

'Nonsense! What utter rubbish are you talking, Mr Mitter?' shouted Mr Bose. 'Where is the proof that I am Dr Vaidya?'

In reply, Feluda asked him a strange question. 'Where is your ring, Mr Bose?'

'My ring?'

'Yes, the one with "Ma" engraved on it. There's a white mark on your finger, but you're not wearing your ring. Where did it go?'

'Oh, that . . .' Mr Bose swallowed. 'I took it off because . . . because it felt too tight.' He took the ring out of his pocket to show us he still had it with him.

'When you changed your make-up and your costume, you forgot to put it back on. I had noticed that mark that evening when you were supposed to be talking to the departed soul of Shelvankar. I found it odd then, but did not pay enough attention at the time.'

Mr Bose began to rise, but Feluda's voice rang out again, cold as steel, 'Don't try to move, Mr Bose. I haven't finished.' Mr Bose quickly sat down again, and began wiping his face. Feluda continued, 'The day after Mr Shelvankar died, Dr Vaidya said he was going to Kalimpong. He didn't. He shed his disguise, became Sasadhar Bose and returned to Calcutta. He had already sent a telegram to Shelvankar saying "Arriving Fourteenth". This upset him very much since Mr Bose wasn't supposed to be in Sikkim at all. Anyway, he came here on the fourteenth just to create an alibi for himself. Then he pretended to be greatly distressed by his partner's death and said he would go back to Bombay the next day. Again, he didn't. He remained in hiding somewhere near Gangtok. He returned as Dr Vaidya just to add to the confusion, and pretend he could speak to the dead. But by then he had come to know that I was a detective. So he tried to remove me from the scene too by throwing another boulder at me. He must have seen me walking towards Nathula Road, and had probably guessed what I was going to do. And it was he who had followed us to Rumtek—' Feluda was interrupted suddenly by a high-pitched wail. To my surprise, I discovered it was coming from Mr Sarkar.

'All right, Mr Sarkar,' said Feluda. 'Out with it! And I want the truth. Why did you go to the spot where the murder had taken place?'

Mr Sarkar raised his hands as though someone had shouted, 'Hands up!' Then he croaked, 'I d-didn't know, you see, how val-valuable that statue was. When they t-told me—'

'Was it you who went to the Tibetan Institute?'

'Yes. They s-said it was totally unique. So I th-thought—'

'So you thought there was no harm in stealing from a dead man if the statue was still lying at the accident site? Especially when it had once belonged to you?'

'Y-yes, something like th-that.'

'But didn't you see anyone at that particular spot?'

'No, sir.'

'All right. But it appears that someone did see you and was afraid that you had seen him. Hence the threats you received.'

'Yes, that explains it.'

'Where's the statue?'

'Statue? But I didn't find it!'

'What? You—?' Feluda was interrupted again, this time by Mr Bose. He jumped to his feet, overturning his chair, and rushed out of the room. Helmut, who was standing at the door, was knocked down by him. Since there was only one door that led to the veranda outside, and this exit was blocked for a few moments by Helmut, who had fallen to the ground, we were delayed by about ten seconds.

By the time all of us could get out, Mr Bose had climbed back into his jeep, and its engine had already roared into life. No doubt his driver had been warned and prepared for such an eventuality. His jeep made a quick about-turn and began moving towards the forest. Without a word, Thondup, who was standing by our own jeep, threw himself back in it and started the engine, assuming we would want to follow Mr Bose. As it turned out, however, there was no need to do that. Feluda took out his revolver from his pocket and fired at the rear wheels of Mr Bose's jeep. The tyres burst instantly, making the jeep tilt to one side, run into a tree, and finally come to a halt. Mr Bose jumped out, and vanished among the trees. His driver came out too, clutching the starting handle of his jeep. Feluda ignored him completely. He ran after Mr Bose, with Helmut, Mr Sarkar and me right behind him. Out of the corner of my eye, I saw Thondup pick up his own starting handle and move forward steadily, to deal with the other driver.

The four of us shot off in different directions to look for Mr Bose. I heard Helmut call out to us about ten minutes later. By the time I found him, Feluda and Mr Sarkar had joined him already. Mr Bose was standing under a large tree a few feet away. No, he wasn't just standing. He was actually hopping around, stamping his feet and wriggling in what appeared to be absolute agony.

The reason became clear as we got closer to him. He had been attacked by leeches. At least two hundred of them were clinging to his body, some on his legs, others on his neck, shoulders and elbows. Helmut pointed at a thick root that ran across the ground near the tree. Obviously, Mr Bose had stumbled against it and fallen flat on the ground.

Feluda caught him by his collar and pulled him out in the open. 'Get those sticks with the bundles of salt and tobacco,' he said to me. 'Quick!'

We had finished eating, and were sitting on the veranda of the dak bungalow. Helmut was taking photographs of orchids. Thondup had gone and informed the police in the nearest town. Mr Bose had been handed over to them. The statue of Yamantak had been found amongst his belongings. He had forgotten to take it from Mr Shelvankar on the day of the murder. He went back later to look for it where the jeep had fallen, and found it behind a bush. As he was climbing up the hill, he saw Mr Sarkar going down, with the same purpose in mind. Fearing that he might have been seen, he started threatening and frightening Mr Sarkar.

It also turned out that Mr Bose had an accomplice in Bombay, with whom he had stayed in touch. It was this man who had answered Feluda's call, received his telegram and informed Mr Bose in Gangtok.

Having explained these details, Feluda turned to Mr Sarkar. 'You are a small-time crook yourself, aren't you? You're lucky you couldn't retrieve that statue. If you had, we'd have had to find a suitable punishment for you.'

'I've been punished adequately, believe me!' Mr Sarkar said, looking profusely apologetic. 'I found as many as three leeches in one of my socks. They must have drunk gallons of my blood. I feel quite weak, as a matter of fact.'

'I see. Anyway, I hope you'll have the sense not to sell anything else that belonged to your grandfather. And look, here's your button.'

I noticed for the first time that the last button on Mr Sarkar's shirt was missing. Mr Sarkar took the button from Feluda and, after a long time, smiled his old smile.

'Th-thanks,' he said.

Read More in the Adventures of Feluda

The House of Death

A mysterious incident in Nepal. A dead body on the beaches of Puri. A murder in an abandoned house . . .

The search for a valuable scroll leads Feluda and his friends to a strange case of characters, and perhaps the most chilling case Feluda has ever been faced with. For among D.G. Sen, the collector of scrolls, his son Mahim, his secretary Nishit, the wildlife photographer Bilas Majumdar and the astrologer Laxman Bhattacharya, there is a cold-blooded criminal, and he must be stopped before it is too late . . . Feluda's twelve greatest adventures are now available in special Puffin editions. This is the eleventh book in the series.

Read More in the Adventures of Feluda

The Bandits of Bombay

A murder in an elevator. A trail of heady perfume. The Nanasaheb's priceless Naulakha necklace . . .

Feluda, Topshe and Jatayu are in Bombay where Jatayu's latest book is being filmed under the title Jet Bahadur. Soon after Jatayu hands over a package to a man in a red shirt, a man is murdered in the elevator of the high-rise where the producer of the film lives. Feluda and his companions find themselves in the midst of one of their most thrilling adventures ever, with a hair-raising climax aboard a train during location shooting.